Cauldrons, Charms & Chai

A COZY ROMANTIC FANTASY NOVEL

TALES FROM THE TAVERN
BOOK THREE

T.L. STONE

BROADMOOR BOOKS

For everyone who's carried something heavy for far too long.

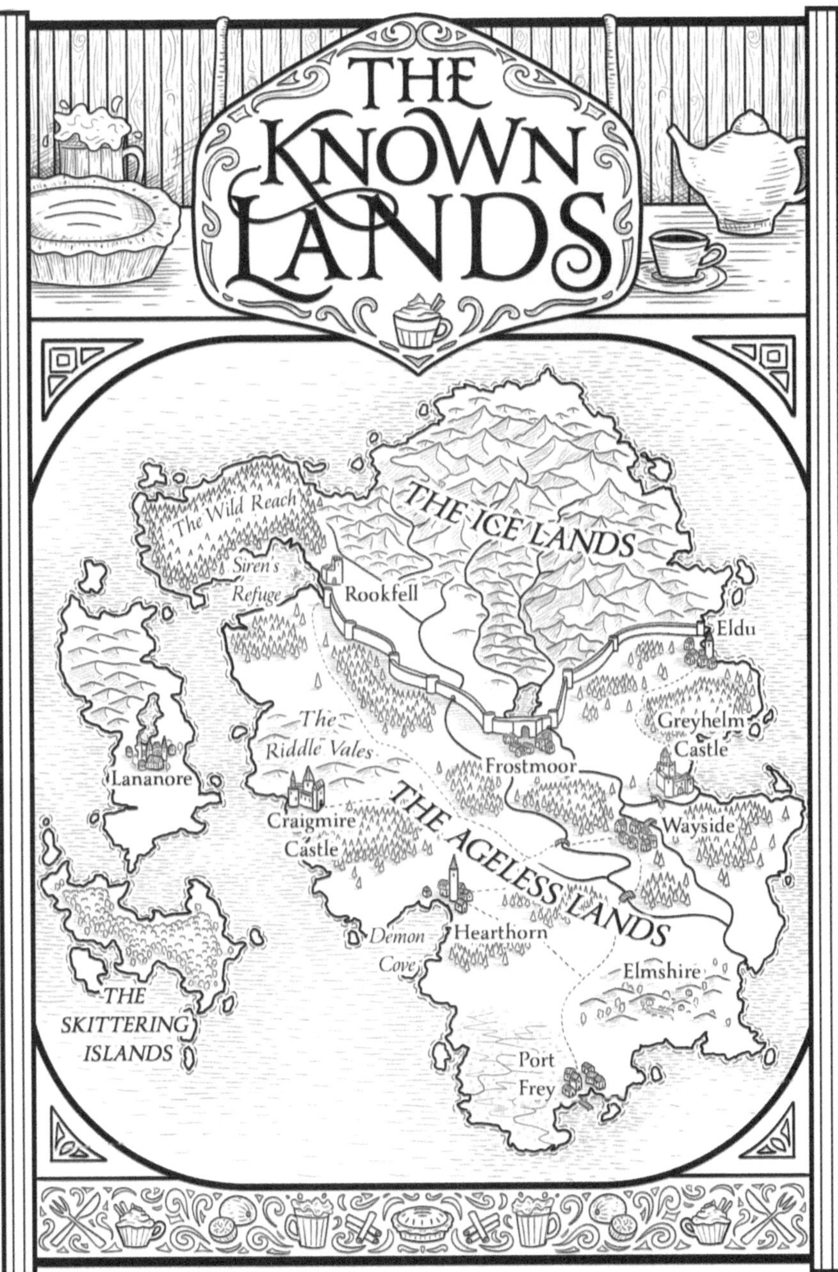

THE KNOWN LANDS
THE ICE LANDS
THE AGELESS LANDS
The Wild Reach
Siren's Refuge
Rookfell
Eldu
Greyhelm Castle
The Riddle Vales
Frostmoor
Wayside
Lananore
Craigmire Castle
Demon Cove
Hearthorn
Elmshire
THE SKITTERING ISLANDS
Port Frey

One

VASKEL RAN a hand over one of his horns, the ridged surface warm despite the snowflakes occasionally landing on it. He let the door to the Wayside Inn close with a sigh behind him as he took in the snowy village that was sluggishly shrugging off the dawn. Birds stayed nestled under eaves dripping with icicles, and thatch roofs huddled under blankets of glistening snow. Smoke curled from chimneys, twisting and spinning into the sullen sky that foretold another snowy day.

The solstice might have passed and the days might be lengthening, but that didn't mean the village wasn't in for more winter. Vaskel rubbed his bare hands together and smiled, invigorated by the cold. To say that the hellkin ran hot would be a vast understatement.

"Thought you'd sneak out without me?"

He turned at the voice from behind, stepping forward as Cali slipped outside with him. The pantheri wore her usual snug-fitting brown leather pants and vest, her bow and a quiver of arrows slung over one shoulder and her gray-striped arms exposed. She also relished the cold, although for her it had to do with her fur and not because she was an infernal being like Vaskel.

"When has anyone ever evaded you?" he asked with a wry grin, as he flipped up the collar of his long cloak.

The archer returned his smile, lifting one shoulder as if acknowledging the truth of this. "If anyone could, it would be you."

His former crew mate knew him just as well as he knew her, and she knew all too well that one of his many talents was stealth, aided by his unnatural ability to sense danger before it reared its head.

"But why would I?" He stepped away from the rustic wooden building, heading for the market stalls that were still in the process of being set up.

Cali fell in step with him, both their tails swinging behind them. "Maybe you have errands for the tavern you want to keep under wraps."

He cocked a brow at her. He had taken over the job of bartender for the village tavern, but his tasks comprised pulling pints, charming the patrons, and keeping the bar clean. "Secret errands?"

She laughed at this. "I suppose not, although Lira might have given you tasks for the wedding."

Now Vaskel chuckled as he stroked one hand down his short beard. "From what I can tell, Lira and Korl aren't the ones in charge of their wedding."

Around them, vendors were shaking snow from fabric awnings that shaded their stalls and farmers were unloading crates jammed with winter vegetables. Even though most vendors weren't open for business, Vaskel enjoyed walking around and eyeing the wares.

Cali clasped her paws behind her as they wound between the stalls, snow crunching beneath their feet. "Tinpin seems to have shifted seamlessly from coordinating the Solstice Festival to arranging Lira's and Korl's wedding."

Vaskel didn't need to remind Cali that the gnome haberdasher had appointed himself to both positions.

"Tin has a strong design aesthetic," Cali said, "but the wedding seems to have taken on a life of its own."

"I don't think her uncle has helped rein it in either."

Cali snorted a laugh. "Don't tell me you're surprised that the elf who travels with a personal staff and lute player veers toward excess." Then the pantheri put a paw on Vaskel's arm. "You don't think he's going to insist on having lute music, do you?"

Vaskel stopped to eye bottles of shimmering, amber honey. "I think lute music is the least of our worries with Erindil."

"You don't think he'll bring Glen to the wedding, do you?" Cali asked, dropping her voice.

Vaskel thought of the scene the ostrich had made during the solstice festival. "As his date? No. Do I put it past him to suggest that Lira ride him for the processional? No."

Cali's golden eyes widened. "Should we step in? I know we're not technically a crew anymore but—"

"Once a crew, always a crew," Vaskel said with more heat than he'd intended.

Her whiskers twitched. "I was going to say that we're family. Not the ones we were born into, perhaps, but the one we chose."

Since hellkin families weren't exactly close, the family Vaskel had formed with his crew mates meant he no longer walked through life alone. It was something he'd never expected, but now couldn't imagine life without.

He exhaled, his breath puffing out in a cloud as he absently rubbed a prickling spot on one wrist. "But now we're a family inside the larger Wayside family."

"Sure, but we've known Lira the longest, aside from Iris. We know what she'd like and what she'd hate."

The mention of Iris made Vaskel's mind wander. He felt like so many of the residents of Wayside had become like family, but Iris was different. The warmth he felt when he looked at her, when she sat at the bar to talk to him late in the evenings, or when he stopped into her apothecary was different that the friendship he felt with Cali or even Lira.

Vaskel was more than aware of his reputation as a seducer. It was part of every hellkin's nature to charm others, male and female alike. His skills had come in handy during years crewing, although it also meant he'd left a trail of bruised hearts in his wake. But once he'd reached Wayside, he'd tucked that part of himself firmly in the past. Then he'd met Iris.

The woman, who was nothing like the young, starry-eyed creatures he typically charmed, had instantly fascinated him. Iris had a past filled with almost as many tales of adventure as he did, and there was no chance empty promises and sultry smiles would ever seduce her. That was what made her all the more fascinating and all the more impossible.

The former rogue and current village apothecary might be his friend, but she'd known enough hellkins in her day to make her immune to his usual techniques of seduction. He'd learned that the hard way and had a shelf in his room filled with remedies and healing oils to show for it.

"Vask?"

He snapped back to reality, blinking at Cali as she repeated his name. He also realized he was scratching his wrist with more than a little vigor.

The pantheri narrowed her eyes at his wrist. "You okay?"

Even though his skin burned beneath his sleeve, he shook it off. "Yes. Sorry. I got distracted by the honey."

Cali crossed her arms as she studied him. "Mmm hmm. Something distracted you." She flicked her gaze toward the apothecary shop, then opened her mouth.

Before she could ask him something he wouldn't want to answer, Vaskel patted her arm and backed away, his mind set on visiting the apothecary before he made his way to The Tusk & Tail. "You might be right about Lira's wedding."

Cali closed her mouth, then opened it again. "Of course, I'm right."

"I should head to the tavern, but I'm glad we're in agreement." He beamed at her. "Let's talk about your plan more tonight."

A myriad of emotions crossed the pantheri's face, finally settling on utter confusion. "What plan?"

"HELLO?" Vaskel eased his head around the opening in the door, his eyes slowly adjusting to the dim interior of the apothecary as he peered inside.

Stepping fully into the shop and wincing at the jangle of the bell overhead, he took in the dark walls lined with shelves and the ebony-glass jars and bottles filling them. Even without reading the paper labels curling at the edges, Vaskel knew the containers held exotic oils and rare ingredients, all of which were used in the various powders and tinctures Iris blended. His nose twitched as he inhaled the cacophony of scents that some found overwhelming, but he found comforting.

"Hello?" The echo of his greeting from deep within the shop was softer and higher-pitched, holding traces of wariness.

Iris's face appeared at the seam of the heavy brown curtains that served as the gateway to the back room, her drowsy expression quickly morphing into a smile. "Vaskel?"

Suddenly, the hellkin was overcome with a bout of uncertainty. "Is it too early?"

Iris stepped through the curtain, shaking her head. "I'm open. I popped back to put the kettle on, that's all."

Vaskel took tentative steps toward the counter separating them. Being unsure of himself was an odd sensation, but Iris rattled him like no one else. It certainly wasn't because of any effort on the woman's part. Despite her adventuring past—a past not everyone knew of and she rarely spoke about—Iris had taken to the role as the village apothecary and de facto healer with enthusiasm.

She wore her silver-streaked dark curls loose or piled on top of her head in a haphazard bun. Her colorful skirts were full, and the half-moon spectacles—ones Vaskel suspected she didn't need— often rested on the tip of her nose, while the distinct blend of scents from her shop clung to her skin like perfume. Despite all this, or perhaps because of it, Vaskel found her fascinating.

Iris leaned her elbows on the counter, steepling her fingers and resting her chin on them. "You're out early."

"Cali and I were in the market," he said, his tongue thick and the words tripping from him in a clumsy muddle.

Iris's gaze took in his lack of bags or market wares, but she didn't comment. Instead, her smile brightened. "Did Cali mention finishing the latest book I lent her?"

Vaskel couldn't keep up with the rate at which Iris supplied his friend with novels and Cali read them. "She didn't, but I think she's given up trying to explain the appeal of pirate romance."

Iris laughed, straightening. "This is technically a mermaid romance, but there are one or two pirates."

Vaskel couldn't help but grin at the woman's laugh, the sound loosening something inside him. "I think you're a big part of why Cali wanted to stay in Wayside. She's never met anyone with as many books as you have."

Iris's green eyes were luminous behind her glasses. "That's one of the reasons I agreed to settle in Wayside all those years ago. I could finally have all the books I'd ever desired." She winked at him. "Running with a crew isn't exactly conducive to building a library."

His chest hitched in response to the wink. That was usually *his* move, but he was sure she hadn't done it in the practiced way he did. Even so, it had knocked him off balance, and he cleared his throat gruffly and tried to remember his excuse for popping into her shop. But her mention of crewing sent his mind skittering to her time as a rogue and her friendship with Lira's gran, who had been their crew's mage. "How long did you—?"

The whistle of a teakettle interrupted his question, and Iris turned away with a bit too much eagerness. "I'd better get that."

Then he was left standing alone in the shop, wondering if there was a reason the apothecary avoided talking about her crewing days or if he was imagining her dodging the topic. Either way, he needed to get a hold of himself, or the woman was going to question his frequent visits. As it was, she probably thought he came down with more than his fair share of throat tickles and sore muscles.

The one thing he refused to ask her about was the only true twinge of pain he'd experienced lately, but if he told the apothecary that the enchanted ring she'd given Sass to warn of danger had prickled when he'd tried it on, that might raise more questions than he wanted. Besides, he had sensed nothing since that single prickle. There was no reason to believe it was anything but a glitch. He thought of his prickling wrist in the market, then quickly dismissed that as a product of the dry air, and more of an itch than a prickle.

When Iris emerged from behind the curtains again, she held two cups of tea. She extended one to him, inclining her head slightly. "This should help with that sore throat you had a few days ago. I added some lemon oil for you."

Vaskel thanked her, cringing inwardly that she'd remembered his last manufactured ailment as he sipped the hot tea that was indeed tangy with lemon.

"How is your throat?" she asked. "Did the herbs help?"

He nodded while swallowing. "It's better than ever." At least that was not a lie. His throat was better than ever, perhaps because it had never been sore.

Iris smiled over the rim of her flowered teacup. "Then you didn't come back for more herbs. What can I help you with today?"

He cursed himself for speaking too quickly. Now he couldn't simply ask for more of the last remedy. If he continued to complain of new aches and pains every time he stopped in to see Iris, she would think he was dancing on death's door. Then he remembered his conversation with Cali.

"Lira's wedding," he blurted.

This made Iris tilt her head. "Lira's wedding?"

He released a breath that sounded more relieved than he would have liked. "Cali and I are worried that the elaborate celebration the village wants to throw might not be what she and Korl want. You've known her longer than anyone, though."

Iris placed her teacup on the counter as she mulled this over. "Tin has a tendency to take charge of celebrations, and Lira doesn't have her gran here to run interference."

"You're as close a thing to family that she has," Vaskel said, "aside from Erindil, but his ideas of a celebration are even more extravagant than Tin's."

Iris scrunched her lips to one side. "That's putting it mildly."

Vaskel pressed on, knowing the one thing to say that would secure Iris's help. "You knew her gran better than anyone. I'm sure Elia would want you to step in for her."

Iris's eyes became glassy, but she sniffed and squared her shoulders. "You're right. I always promised Elia I would look out for Lira. She would want me to make sure Lira's wedding is about what she wants."

Vaskel felt a stab of guilt that he pushed aside as he realized what he'd said was true. If there was anyone who could ensure that Lira's wedding didn't become a spectacle, it was Iris.

"I'm glad you stopped in this morning, Vaskel." Iris drained the last of her tea and held his gaze. "I'll stop by the tavern this evening to talk to her."

Vaskel downed his remaining tea in a single gulp before wishing Iris farewell and already eagerly anticipating her visit that evening. It wasn't until he stepped outside the shop doors that his mind cleared enough for him to notice that the prickling on his wrist had shifted from mildly irritating to impossible to ignore.

Three

VASKEL WIPED down the bar with more force than strictly necessary, the worn wood gleaming under his crimson fingers. He'd been eyeing the door all night, but so far, there had been no sign of Iris. He gave an absent rub of his tingling wrist and busied himself pulling a pint for a bandy-legged sailor who was a long way from port.

Sliding the tankard across the bar and scooping up the dingy copper bits in return, Vaskel cast his gaze across the tavern's great room that hummed with comfortable chaos. Warmth radiated from the massive stone hearth, flames spewing shadows across the rough-hewn beams overhead. The air was thick with the scents of cinnamon, peat, and Lira's latest batch of meat pies cooling in the kitchen. Underneath it all lingered the familiar tang of ale and the sweetness of mulled wine that had become the drink of choice as the nights had gotten colder.

Sass sauntered toward him with a tray balanced on one hand, her dark braid swinging and her ample hips swaying. The dwarf had become an expert at weaving her way through the crowded tables, dodging flailing arms and close-pressed bodies without breaking stride. But even she blew out a breath when she reached him, tucking a cloth into the waistband of her brown skirt.

"Another round of ale for the table in the corner." She flicked her dark eyes toward the kitchen doors. "Any word on fresh meat pies?"

Vaskel shrugged. He knew better than to poke his head into Lira's kitchen and ask. Being hurried did nothing but make her glower these days. "Why don't you ask the bride-to-be?"

Sass snorted a laugh. "I prefer to keep my head, thank you very much." Then she lowered her voice. "You don't think her recent moodiness is wedding jitters, do you? You don't think she's having second thoughts?"

Vaskel glanced at the stone fireplace where Korl occupied one of the oversized armchairs, the orc's massive form making the furniture look like it belonged in a child's nursery. He was sketching something on a piece of parchment, probably a design for a new gadget. Vaskel thought about how the guard-turned-tinker had courted Lira by making her a new stove, and a smile tugged at his lips.

"I don't think she's having second thoughts about Korl," he said with a shake of his head.

"Aye." Sass nodded. "You're right. She adores the big, green lug."

Vaskel grinned at this, knowing that Sass's barbs were terms of endearment. "And how's your big, blonde lug?"

Sass tried to wrestle away a pleased look as she cleared her throat. "I don't know if she's mine. It's not like *we're* the ones engaged."

The broad-shouldered guardswoman sat in her usual chair across from Korl, knitting needles clicking in a steady rhythm. Val held up what appeared to be the beginning of a white wool scarf, catching Sass's eyes and grinning.

"Not yet," Vaskel teased before squinting at the knitting. "Another scarf?"

"Scarves are her specialty." There was both pride and a hint of defensiveness in the dwarf's voice. "This one is for the wedding."

"Could be a table runner if Lira doesn't want to wear a scarf down the aisle," Vaskel suggested, avoiding a sharp look from Sass.

"Scarves are what she does best," Sass blew a loose curl off her forehead. "Well, that and swinging a sword."

Vaskel chuckled as he retrieved a clean tankard from beneath the bar and began filling it with dark ale. "Speaking of those with a fondness for weapons, have you seen Thrain?"

Sass swept her gaze across the great room, wrinkling her nose when it didn't land on her childhood friend. "He's probably sleeping off last night's apple brandy drink-off with Rog."

"That explains why the gnome isn't here."

Rog was another of Vaskel and Lira's former crew who'd found his way to the village, along with his brandy-brewing wife, Rosie.

"They aren't the only ones who might need to sleep it off." Sass gestured with her head to one of the long tables. "Pip, Fenni, and Tin are having a rather heated debate about whether sugar-work sculptures are the best centerpieces."

As if summoned by the mention of their names, the three villagers' voices rose from their table.

"Sugar work is an art form!" Pip insisted, his wiry hair still dusted with flour although he'd left his bakery long ago. "I can create snowflakes you would swear are real!"

"But sugar is very fragile, brother." The halfling cheesemonger patted his brother's chubby hand. "And you have enough work to do just baking the wedding cake."

Pip frowned at this, but bobbled his head in tacit acknowledgement of a good point. "The cake *will* be spectacular."

"That's why fabric is the perfect alternative." Tinpin adjusted his emerald cravat, and his long, pointed gnome's cap flopped to one side. "Perfect, I tell you. Silk snowflakes will never shatter. Never, never."

"They've been at it for an hour," Sass said with a wicked grin as she plopped the full tankards on her tray and backed away from him. "I'm half tempted to suggest ice sculptures just to watch them unite against a common enemy."

Vaskel laughed, glad for the distraction from his impatience. The contentment had barely settled in his bones when the tavern door burst open, bringing with it a blast of winter air that made everyone near the entrance yelp and huddle deeper into their cloaks and shawls.

Cali strode inside, her gray fur speckled with snowflakes, making her look momentarily spotted. The pantheri shook herself from her pointed ears to the tip of her striped tail, sending droplets of melted snow flying.

She pushed back her hood. "It's really coming down out there."

Behind her, Iris emerged, hidden beneath a heavy cloak. The village apothecary brushed off some of Cali's scattered snowflakes before tossing back her hood and revealing her mass of curls teased with glints of silver. Her violet and orange patchwork skirt jingled as she walked to the bar and slid onto a stool, while Cali hurried to warm her fur by the fire.

Vaskel gave the apothecary his most charming smile, the one that had gotten him out of (and occasionally into) trouble across half the Known Lands, and hoped she couldn't tell how relieved he was to see her. "I thought the snow might have kept you away."

She rubbed her hands together and shook her head. "I'll admit that it delayed me and that it was tempting to stay curled up in a chair at home." She gave him an amiable smile. "But a promise is a promise. Now, do you have any of that mulled wine?"

He pivoted to an earthenware pitcher, pouring a generous amount into a pewter goblet and sliding it across the bar to her. His gaze tracked the delicate way she wrapped her fingers around the stem, and when the tips of his fingers brushed hers, a tingle sent heat sliding up his hand. He pulled back, rubbing his fingers and wondering if the apothecary possessed magic, after all.

Iris seemed unaffected as she took a sip and sighed. "Perfect."

Vaskel smiled, but his attention was almost instantly hijacked, and it wasn't from the pleasant buzz of her touch. The prickling sensation had returned, the one he'd first felt months ago when he'd worn Iris's charmed ring that signaled danger, and again that morning. But this time there was no ring to blame.

His hand moved involuntarily to his wrist, rubbing at the spot where his sleeve met his hand. The sensation was an insistent itch that seemed to pulse in time with his heartbeat.

Not now, he thought, forcing his hand back to the bar.

But even as he tried to dismiss it, the sensation intensified. The prickle that had started as a faint murmur beneath his skin was now emerging as something darker and more insistent.

"Vaskel?" Iris's voice cut through his thoughts. "Are you unwell?"

He dredged up a grin, the kind that had fooled guards and maidens alike. "A bit tired is all."

But as he reached for an empty tankard from farther down the bar, his sleeve shifted, and he glimpsed his wrist. His breath lurched in his throat.

There, barely visible against his skin, were marks. Dark lines that hadn't been there this morning curled up from his wrist like smoke rendered in flesh. They were so faint he might have dismissed them as tricks of the firelight, but he knew better. He'd seen marks like these before.

The tankard slipped from his suddenly nerveless fingers, clattering on the bar and splattering warm dregs of ale. Several patrons looked up, but Sass was already there with a cloth, tsk-ing at him good-naturedly.

"Butter-fingers tonight, are we?" she said, but her expression was concerned. "You feeling all right, Vask?"

"Just weary," he managed, pulling his sleeve down as far as it would go. "It's been a long day."

Sass didn't look convinced, but a call for ale from another table drew her back to the great room. It was Iris who didn't look away, her dubious gaze following him as he attempted to go about his work.

The last time he'd seen dark marks etched in skin, the wearer had been consumed by dark magic. Dark magic that had rebounded on him. But Vaskel hadn't been playing with magic of any kind.

The hellkin twitched as he thought back to that night on the cliffs. He had been in close contact with the dark magic. Could the marks have infected him? He shook his head, as if to dislodge the thought. He'd been fine for months, shown no signs, felt nothing unusual except...

Except for that prickling when he'd worn Iris's ring that warned of danger. What if the danger it had been warning him about was himself? What if he was infected with dark magic?

"Vask?" Lira's voice made him jump. She stood in the kitchen doorway, her auburn hair dusted with flour, worry pleating her brow. "Sass said you're not feeling well. Do you need to take a break? We can handle the bar."

"I'm fine," he said, perhaps too quickly. "Just tired and overheated."

Lira arched a brow at this. A hellkin too warm? Luckily, she didn't call him on it.

"Go," she said. "Get some fresh air."

"That's right." Sass came behind the bar and used a dishtowel to shoo him away. "I can cover the bar for a bit. You take a breather."

He mumbled thanks, grabbed his cloak from the peg behind the bar, tromped woodenly across the great room, and stepped out into the snowy night. The cold was biting, but he welcomed it. Maybe it would clear his head and help him think.

The snow cavorted in thick, lazy flakes through the night air, and his breath formed clouds in the cold as he pulled back his sleeve. The marks were clearer in the warm spill of light from the lantern over the door, winding around his wrist in delicate spirals, like ink traced beneath his skin.

"Hells and cinders," he muttered, the pointed tip of his tail quivering like it often did when danger was approaching.

Behind him, the tavern door opened, gushing golden light and laughter into the darkness. He quickly yanked down his sleeve and turned to see Iris stepping out, wrapped in her heavy cloak.

"I thought you might need this," she said, offering him a steaming mug. "Lira's chai."

He accepted it gratefully and let the warmth seep into his fingers. "Thank you."

The apothecary bustled the front of her cloak together with one hand, the icy air clearly not as welcome for her. "Would you like to talk about it?"

For a moment, he considered telling her everything. Iris had been an adventurer herself once, after all. But the words died in his throat. What could he say? That he was cursed with dark magic? He didn't even know that for sure. "It's nothing."

Iris studied him for a long moment, a shadow of a smile playing across her face, and he had the uncomfortable feeling she saw right through his lie. But she only patted his arm. "Maybe it's that sore throat returning."

He met her gaze, not sure if she was calling him out for all his feigned illnesses, but her expression betrayed nothing. "Maybe."

She jerked her head toward the tavern door. "I'm going to have a chat with Lira about the wedding. You stay outside as long as you need."

She rested her hand on his arm, and for a moment, the heat of her touch masked the prickling of his skin. Then she gave a quick squeeze and slipped back into the tavern, leaving him alone with the cascading snow and his swirling thoughts.

Vaskel stood under the creaking wooden tavern sign for a long while, watching the light from the leaded windows paint golden squares on the icy ground and trying to come up with explanations for his marks.

Every single one made his blood run cold.

Four

THE HEAVY WOODEN door thudded shut after the last patron stumbled outside, and Sass thunked a pair of tankards on the bar. "All clear!"

The kitchen doors swung open, and Lira emerged with Crumpet perched on her shoulder, the flutterstoat's white fur dusted with what looked suspiciously like cinnamon. The half-elf's auburn hair had come loose from its bun, wisps of it decorated with flour, and there was a buttery smudge on her cheek.

"Tomorrow morning's crumpets are ready," she announced,

stretching her arms overhead with a satisfied groan. The winged stoat chittered, his tiny wings fluttering as he groomed flour from his whiskers.

"About time you emerged from your baking cave," Cali said, as she helped flip chairs on top of tables, the pantheri's tail swishing languidly. "I was beginning to think you'd been buried under an avalanche of dough."

"Nearly was," Lira admitted with a laugh, making her way to the fire. She sank onto Korl's lap with obvious relief, and Crumpet immediately relocated to her lap, curling into a contented ball. The orc wrapped his arms around his fiancé, comforting her without saying a word.

Sass finished her sweeping, wrapped up the sea shanty she'd been humming, and propped the broom against the wall before joining them and pulling up a chair. "You know your wedding is all anyone's talking about."

Lira sighed. "It's turned into a village project."

"You can't blame them, love," Iris said. "Two of Wayside's own getting married? One of whom vanished for years before returning."

Lira rolled her eyes but snuggled against Korl. "I didn't vanish, and I did come home."

"Even though the entire town is excited about your wedding," Iris said, as she swung a finger between Lira and Korl, "it's still yours."

"Is it?" Lira asked with a weary exhale that Vaskel suspected came from more than hours in the kitchen.

Iris crossed to Lira and rested a hand on her shoulder. "It is, so if it's turning into something you don't want, we can fix that."

Lira looked up at the woman, her lips quirking. "We as in...?"

Cali joined Iris and threw a gray striped arm around her shoulders. "All of us."

Lira laughed. "It might take all of you to talk Pip out of a five-tier cake."

"Who said the cake was a bad idea?" Sass asked, jutting out one hip. "Dwarves can eat a lot of cake, and now there are two of us."

"So one tier for you and one for Thrain?" Cali asked.

Sass smiled wryly. "If it's Pip's cake we're talking about, that sounds about right."

Even Korl laughed at this, and Vaskel grinned from the bar, glad to see Lira smiling about her wedding plans. Maybe she wasn't as nervous about it as he and Cali had suspected.

He listened to their continued wedding talk with half an ear as he polished the bar top, the familiar motion soothing even as the marks on his arm seemed to seethe beneath his flesh. He'd avoided thinking about them for the past hour, losing himself in the routine of closing work, but now that he was almost done, it was hard to ignore the burning sensation.

Crumpet's snores carried all the way to the bar, making Vaskel glance up.

Cali laughed as she stretched her slender arms overhead. "He has the right idea. I should head back to the inn before the snow starts again." She glanced at the window where frost had crept up the glass in delicate patterns. "You coming, Vask?"

"I have to do a few more things. You go without me."

Cali shrugged, then slipped out into the night, letting in a flurry of frigid air that made the fire flicker and its shadows lap the ceiling. Sass yawned enormously, not bothering to cover her mouth.

"Right then, I'm off to bed too," the dwarf announced as she stood. "I should save my energy for the wedding festivities."

"It's a wedding, not a bacchanal," Lira said.

Sass brushed a loose brown curl from her eyes. "Dwarf wedding celebrations last days, and the hangovers last even longer."

"Good thing we aren't dwarves," Korl said, his words rumbling low and husky.

"You should be so lucky," Sass called over her shoulder as she headed for the stairs to the second floor of the tavern and her bedroom. "'Night all. Don't stay up too late."

That left Lira, Korl, Iris, and Vaskel in the quiet tavern. Lira carefully transferred the sleeping Crumpet from her lap to Korl's as she stood.

"I should give the kitchen a final once-over before we go," she said, though her movements were slow and her voice laden with exhaustion.

"Go home," Vaskel told her from behind the bar. "The kitchen is fine. I'll check it for you if you want, but you should get some rest."

Lira gave him a grateful smile. "What would I do without you?"

"You'd have a less charming bartender," he said lightly, though something twisted in his chest at her trust.

"So true. Durn wasn't exactly drawing crowds." Lira crinkled her nose at the memory of the old, grumpy tavernkeep before a yawn split her face. She crossed to the door and pulled her cloak off the hook. "Night, Vask. Night, Iris." She smiled at the apothecary. "You sure you'll be safe from Vaskel's charm?"

Iris laughed. "Oh, I think I can resist the blue-eyed hellkin's wiles."

Vaskel attempted to ignore the warmth seeping up his neck at Iris's teasing tone and the fact that the same words by anyone else wouldn't make his pulse nearly as jumpy.

Korl gathered the still-sleeping Crumpet in his arms and headed into the kitchen, presumably tucking the creature into his nest of dishtowels. Then he emerged through the half-doors, took Lira's hand, and led her out. That left Vaskel and Iris alone in the great room, the fire crackling softly.

Vaskel continued polishing the bar, aware of Iris watching him from her chair by the hearth. After a moment, she rose and made her way to one of the bar stools.

"You know," she said, "I've lived long enough to recognize when someone's carrying a burden they're afraid to share."

Vaskel's hand stilled on the cloth he was using to polish the wood. "I don't know what you mean."

"Of course not," Iris said. "Just like I don't know why you keep tugging at your left sleeve or why you've been avoiding looking at your wrist all evening."

He looked up sharply to find her green eyes studying him with a mixture of concern and understanding. There was no judgment there, only patient waiting.

"It's nothing," he said automatically.

"'Nothing' doesn't make a hellkin's brow pinch."

Vaskel dropped the cloth and braced both hands on the bar. He'd faced down dragons, angry mages, and more bar fights than he could count, but somehow the apothecary's quiet concern undid him.

"You can't tell Lira," he said finally, his voice barely above a whisper.

"That depends entirely on what you're about to show me, but I've seen many strange things in my years, and very little shocks me anymore."

Vaskel hesitated for another long moment, then slowly pushed up his sleeve. The marks were darker now than they'd been earlier and they curved fully around his wrist.

Iris went still. Then, without asking permission, she reached across the bar and took his wrist in her hands. Her touch was warm and surprisingly steady, and Vaskel's heart seized.

"How long?" she asked quietly, her fingers tracing just above the marks without quite touching them.

"I noticed them tonight, but I think they might have started earlier. When I returned the ring to you, I slipped it on. It was only for a moment, but it prickled my skin."

"The ring only warns of danger," Iris murmured, her gaze locked on the marks. "It couldn't have made these."

"Could it be from dark magic? The last time I saw marks like these, they were on Malek."

Iris was silent, her fingers still ghosting over the marks. She knew who Malek was, who he'd been to Vaskel and Lira. She also knew how dangerous he'd been. Then she carefully released his wrist and met his eyes.

"Come to the apothecary tomorrow."

"Can you help?" He hated how desperate he sounded, especially since Iris wasn't a mage.

Even in her crewing days, she'd been a rogue. She'd opened an apothecary shop as a cover when she and Lira's gran had settled in Wayside. Her shop peddled herbs for healing, not magical cures.

"I need to consult some of my books." She stood, sliding her glasses to the tip of her nose. "Tomorrow, Vaskel. And try not to worry too much tonight."

"Easy for you to say," he muttered, dragging his sleeve back down.

She paused at the door, glancing back at him. "You're not Malek. Whatever these marks are, wherever they came from, you're not him. Remember that."

Then she was gone, leaving Vaskel alone in the tavern with the dying fire and the spreading marks on his arm. He looked down at his wrist where her fingers had traced above the dark lines, and he could still feel the warmth of her touch, the spark that had passed between them.

When he finally doused all the candles, smothered the fire, and stepped from the darkened tavern into the cold, the spark he'd felt at Iris's touch hadn't faded.

Five

VASKEL STOOD outside the apothecary as dawn broke the next morning, eyeing its black-and-white striped awning that sagged with snow. The windows were dark, but Iris had told him to come early, before the village stirred, and he trusted she'd be waiting. Besides, he'd spent a restless night tormented by the spreading marks and his own worry.

The hellkin held his breath as he tried the door, but it gave way with a barely audible creak, the bell above the door chiming softly as he entered. Immediately, the familiar aroma of oils and herbs enveloped him, but he also detected the whiff of toasted bread.

"Back here," Iris's voice was muffled from behind the velvet curtains.

Vaskel ducked through and into the book-lined room that was chaos given form. Books topped on every surface, empty teacups bobbled atop teetering stacks, and a massive, gilded cage held hundreds of tiny bookwyrms on swinging perches.

"Don't want them disturbing us," Iris said as she followed his gaze to the towering ceiling above them, usually filled with the tiny creatures that looked like a cross between hummingbirds and baby dragons. "Not today."

That's when Vaskel noticed what sat on the round table in the center of the room. Lira's grandmother's spell book lay open, its pages yellowed with spidery, faded script spooled out across them. But more startling was the cauldron hunched beside it, small and black.

"Is that...?" Vaskel gestured at the cauldron, unable to keep the surprise from his voice.

Iris mustered a smile. "The biggest container I could find. Sometimes the old ways are the best ways, even if they're a touch theatrical." She moved to the table, her flowered skirt swishing. "I may have borrowed this from Lira's kitchen last night when she wasn't looking." She tapped the open spellbook. "She won't mind. Probably."

Vaskel raised an eyebrow. "Probably?"

"If she knew it was for a good cause, Lira wouldn't hesitate to lend me the book. But since you'd rather keep this between us, I thought it better to ask forgiveness instead of permission." Iris began adding ingredients to the cauldron from various bottles and pouches arranged on the table. A pinch of something that sparkled, three drops of liquid that seemed to absorb light rather than reflect it, and a handful of dried leaves that released a burst of rose perfume.

"You know what you're doing?" Vaskel asked as he stepped closer and peered into the cauldron.

Iris didn't even glance up. "This is the same revealing spell that Erindil used on Sass's amulet." She stirred the mixture with a silver spoon that left trails of light in the liquid. "Now then, push up your sleeve and hold your arm over the cauldron. Don't touch the liquid. It won't hurt you, but it might tingle unpleasantly."

Vaskel did as instructed, shoving his sleeve past his elbow to reveal the full extent of the marks. In the pale sunrise peeking through the skylight, they were sinewy ribbons roiling beneath his skin.

Iris murmured words in what might have been Elvish, her voice taking on a rhythm that seemed to hum in Vaskel's bones. The liquid in the cauldron glowed, first amber like firelight, then shifting to deep purple. Then the marks on his arm glowed in response.

They lit up like lines of blue ice edged with silver, the spirals and curves writhing under his skin, and despite how cold they appeared, they burned like fiery flames. Vaskel jerked his arm back, rubbing the skin to stop the scorch.

Iris went still as the light faded from the cauldron. Then she turned to the spell book, flipping through several pages one way, then reversing and flipping many more pages the other. She ran a finger down a list, finally tapping it and sighing. "That's not what I expected."

"What? What is it?"

"It's not dark magic residue," Iris said slowly, looking up from the pages. "If the book is right, what you're carrying is an infernal soul bind."

The words almost made Vaskel stagger back. He knew what a soul bind was—every hellkin did. They were contracts written in flesh and spirit, bonds that tied one infernal being to another until death or a promise fulfilled.

"It can't be," he said, though even as the words left his mouth, he knew they were hollow.

Iris tilted her head, studying him with sharp eyes that seemed to see too much. "Are you sure? A soul bind has to be agreed upon. This couldn't have been placed on you like a curse."

Vaskel groaned, rubbing a hand over his face and the bunched wrinkles of his brow. Of course. Of bloody course. He'd been a fool to think he could outrun the mistakes of his past. Even if he'd changed his ways, his past clearly wasn't done with him.

"Goblin's spawn," he muttered, remembering precisely who he'd made a deal with all those years ago.

He looked down at the marks, no longer glowing but still visible, still spreading, still claiming more of him with each passing hour.

One thing he knew with gut-churning certainty. This was only the beginning.

Six

TWENTY YEARS *earlier*

The shabby tavern reeked of fetid ale, dripping beef tallow, and too many unwashed bodies. Near the Wild Reach, hygiene was more suggestion than requirement, and The Frozen Fang attracted the sort of clientele who considered bathing an annual inconvenience at best.

Shadows and cobwebs coated the corners of the great room, and a crumbling hearth yawned cold and empty along one wall. The muddle of dubious conversations drowned out the scuttling of insects across the grimy floors, even as a mangy dog lurked around the tables hunting for scraps.

Vaskel sat in the corner, nursing his third tankard of something that claimed to be ale. His horns had not reached full-length, marking him as barely past fifty. Orc's blood, he was practically an adolescent by hellkin standards. Infernal creatures didn't live as long as elves, but it wasn't unusual for them to notch a few hundred years under their belts. It also wasn't unusual for them to frequent places like The Frozen Fang, where the law had less of a hold and their kind wasn't such an oddity.

The crew he'd joined two months ago sprawled around a scarred wooden table in various states of intoxication. They weren't the noble band of adventurers he'd dreamed of joining when he'd left the sulfur peaks of his homeland. These were mercenaries, pure and simple, and not even very good ones. They took the jobs others wouldn't touch, asked no questions, and split the gold evenly. It wasn't honorable work, but it paid well, and payment meant survival.

"Another round?" The purr of Marina's voice cut through his brooding thoughts.

She stood beside their table, having appeared without warning, a trait that made Vaskel's tail twitch nervously. Marina was powerful, confident, and devastatingly seductive, everything Vaskel aspired to be. Her crimson horns curved back from her forehead in elegant spirals, signaling that she had passed the age of maturity, and her eyes were a hypnotic shade of violet.

"Always," growled Thork, their orc leader, already deep in his cups.

The one-eyed dwarf, who made the last member of their foursome, belched instead of answering, staggering to his feet and ambling off to bed, leaving only Vaskel, Thork, and Marina in the tavern's smoky common room.

Marina signaled the barkeep with a languid gesture, and a barmaid appeared with foam-topped tankards as if by magic. It could have been magic, knowing Marina. She had abilities that went beyond the natural hellkin talents and powers that made even hardened mercenaries step carefully around her.

Thork lasted another two rounds before his head hit the table with a resounding thunk, snores following immediately after. Marina watched him with amused contempt, then turned her piercing gaze on Vaskel.

"Still awake, little brother?" She always called him that, though they shared no blood. It was a hellkin custom, with older ones often taking the younger under wing, teaching them the ways of their kind in a world that feared and misused them.

"Still thinking," Vaskel corrected, though the ale had made his thoughts pleasantly fuzzy around the edges.

"Dangerous habit in our line of work." She moved to sit beside him, close enough that he could smell the cinnamon and sulfur scent that hewed to her skin. "What troubles you?"

Vaskel hesitated, then the ale made him honest. "The job today. We were supposed to retrieve stolen goods, but those weren't thieves we killed. They were just people trying to protect their possessions."

Marina's laugh was like breaking glass. "Oh, sweet little brother. Still clinging to notions of good and evil? There's only survival and power in this world. Everything else is a pretty story told to children."

"But—"

"You want to survive, don't you?" She leaned closer, her breath warm against his ear. "You want to become powerful enough that no one can ever hurt you, use you, punish you for simply being you?"

The words hit too close to home. Too many had automatically viewed Vaskel as evil for him not to feel the impact of what she said. Here, at least, he was earning his keep, building a reputation, and becoming someone who mattered. Even if the methods made him uneasy.

"Of course," he admitted, the words rasping from his tight jaw.

Marina pulled back enough to study his face, and something calculating flickered in her expression. "You know, I could help with that. Give you an edge that would make you invaluable to any crew. Maybe even let you lead your own one day."

Vaskel's breath snagged in his chest. "What kind of edge?"

"The same one I have." She held up a hand, and light seemed to dance around her fingers despite the tavern's shadows. "The ability to sense danger before it arrives. To know when someone means you harm, when a situation is about to go sideways, when death is reaching for you with icy fingers."

It sounded too good to be true, which in Vaskel's limited experience meant it probably was. "What's the cost?"

Marina smiled, and this time it reached her eyes, making them glow with inner fire. "Clever boy. There's always a cost, isn't there?" She traced a finger along his arm, leaving a trail of warmth that seemed to sink beneath his skin. "Just a simple bind that will link us together and allow my powers to flow to you. Think of it as insurance."

"Insurance?"

"That you won't use the gift against me, of course." Her tone was light, teasing. "And perhaps, one day, far in the future, I might need a favor. Something small. Probably nothing at all. I might never even collect."

Vaskel knew he should ask more questions. Should demand specifics. Should probably run from the tavern and never look back. But the ale made him bold, and the heady promise of power made him lightheaded, and Marina's presence made him want to prove himself.

"How does it work?" he asked.

Marina's smile widened. "Just give me your hand and say that you agree. That's all. It's as simple as breathing."

She extended her hand, palm up, waiting. In the dim tavern

light, her crimson skin seemed to glow as if illuminated from within.

Vaskel looked at her hand and saw his future spreading before him. A special power would make him valuable, powerful, and needed. Like Marina. He placed his hand in hers.

"Do you agree to the binding?" She traced one finger languidly up his arm. "Do you take these powers and this connection?"

"Yes," he said before his brain could talk him out of it.

The moment the word left his lips, pain lanced through his arm like liquid fire. He bit back a scream, not wanting to show weakness, as something seemed to burrow beneath his skin, flames licking the path Marina had traced. The sensation lasted only seconds, but when Marina released him, he could have sworn he saw faint marks on his skin, whispers of black slipping away beneath the red. But when he looked again, there was nothing. Only his skin, unmarked and unblemished.

"Was that so hard, little brother?" Marina asked, her words a velvet caress. "You'll start feeling it within a few days. A prickling sensation when danger approaches. The closer the threat, the stronger the warning. Use it wisely."

She rose gracefully, leaving coins on the table for the ale. "Oh, and Vaskel? Best not to mention this to anyone. They might get jealous, and jealousy leads to such unpleasant complications in our line of work."

He nodded before he noticed her taking her pack from the back of the chair. "You're leaving?"

Her smile unfurled slow and sultry. "It's time for me to fly solo for a while. Besides, two hellkins with the ability to sense danger in a crew would be overkill, don't you think?"

She was gone before he could respond, slipping through the crowd and vanishing into the night. Vaskel sat alone in the tavern, staring at his unmarked arm, wondering what he'd just done.

"It's nothing," he told himself, as his mouth creaked into a yawn. "I'll probably never see her again."

Seven

VASKEL STARED at his arm now, those marks suddenly not unfamiliar or inexplicable. He should have known the moment he saw them. He should have remembered his promise from so many decades ago. But, in his defense, he hadn't seen her since that night.

He'd trekked all over The Known Lands, going from crew to crew and village to village, but he'd never spotted Marina again. He'd never even heard about a beautiful hellkin with special abilities. At first, he'd asked. The first few years after she'd left, he'd looked.

But Marina had proven herself to be as elusive as ever, leaving behind only whispers and tales that seemed too fantastical to be true. After a while, Vaskel convinced himself it had never even happened. Maybe he'd imagined her entirely, he'd thought. He almost laughed at how foolish that idea had been. Foolish and wishful.

Vaskel met Iris's eyes. "I know who's behind this."

The words came out flat and emotionless, but inside Vaskel felt like he might shatter into a thousand pieces. How could he have been so stupid? How could he ever have been so young and reckless and desperate for approval?

Iris studied him. "Someone from your past, I take it?"

Vaskel laughed, but there was no humor in it. "Someone I thought was gone. Someone I hoped was gone. We parted ways years ago, and I parted ways with her kind of work and her way of thinking not long after that." His mind went to Lira and the honorable crew that had become his genuine family. "It was a lifetime ago, and a part of me thought that shedding that version of myself would mean shedding all of it."

He trailed off, staring at the marks. They were more visible now, as if the revealing spell had somehow strengthened them. Or perhaps whoever was on the other end of the soul bind was drawing closer. "I was clearly wrong."

"According to the spell book, soul binds can lie dormant for decades," Iris said. "Sometimes they're never activated."

"I think I always knew this one would be," Vaskel whispered.

The hellkin thought of all the years that had passed since that night in the tavern. He'd changed so much, he'd become someone he could be proud of, and he'd found friends worth keeping. He'd built a good, honest life in Wayside, but now his past was coming to claim its due.

"Twenty years," he said, more to himself than to Iris. He kicked the leg of the table hard enough to make the cauldron jump, and the book-wyrms leapt from their perches and fluttered around the cage. "I was so young then. I didn't understand what I was agreeing to, and I didn't have the first clue about debts and the people who collect them."

"Then you were manipulated," Iris said firmly. "Whoever did this took advantage of your youth and inexperience. That's not foolishness, Vaskel. That's being a victim of someone's cruelty."

But Vaskel barely heard her. He was too busy cursing his younger self, the desperate boy who'd wanted so badly to matter that he'd sold a piece of himself for powers. But if he was being completely truthful, he had little room for complaint. She hadn't tricked him into a poor bargain, and until that moment, he hadn't regretted making the deal. Since so long had passed without a single sign of Marina, it had felt like a bargain that had cost him nothing.

On top of that, the gift Marina had given him had worked. He could sense danger, and he had saved his crew countless times over the years with his warnings. It had made him sought after and valued, even after he'd matured into a fierce fighter in his own right. But now he knew all of that hadn't been free, although he didn't know what it would cost him or why she was collecting now.

Now that he was finally happy. Now that he'd finally found a place to call home. But maybe that was it. Maybe that was why she was calling in her debt. Maybe she knew. Maybe she'd always known precisely where he was. Maybe she'd been biding her time and waiting for the moment when collecting the debt would cost him most dearly.

"There's no doubt in my mind who's behind this," he said, the name sitting like poison on his tongue, a curse he could barely bring himself to utter.

Eight

"MARINA," he said, the name hanging in the air between them. "She was a hellkin I once crewed with, and she's the one..."

Iris reached for his hand when his words faltered, her fingers cool and steady as they wrapped around his. "You don't have to tell me, Vask."

Her touch steadied him, but it also caused his heart to lurch. The contact should have been comforting, but something electric sparked between them that had nothing to do with the soul bind spreading its dark tendrils up his arms.

"I'll figure out how to break this," she promised, her green eyes holding his with an intensity that made his chest constrict. "We've dealt with curses before."

Vaskel's tail, usually so controlled, curled involuntarily around the leg of the stool as the marks beneath his shirt crept up his skin like ivy made of shadow and fire. It wasn't the marks that concerned him most in this moment, though. It was the way Iris's thumb brushed across his knuckles, absent and gentle, as if she wasn't even aware she was doing it.

"Iris..." Her name felt wrenched from his throat.

She looked at him, dark curls framing her face. Her pulse fluttered visibly at the base of her throat, and he leaned closer without meaning to. In that moment, she wasn't the apothecary who'd been best friends with Lira's gran, and he wasn't an infernal being decades older than her.

The warm, exotic scent of her wrapped around him like a potent spell. For a heartbeat, he let himself imagine what it would be like to close the distance between them and unearth the answers to questions he'd always had about the mysterious woman. To let his fingers tangle in her curls and his lips brush the pale skin of her throat.

Then he remembered Marina, and the thought was a bucket of ice water over his head. If Marina truly was behind these marks, if she'd found him, then anyone close to him was in danger. Especially someone Marina might see as a threat to her claim.

He jerked his hand away and stepped back. Her eyes widened slightly, confusion and something that might have been hurt flashing across her features before she smoothed them away and busied herself tidying her herbs and oils.

"Thank you." He backed away so quickly that he nearly upended a stack of books. "I should go before Lira and Sass miss me."

Iris nodded, wrapping her arms around herself as if warding

off a sudden chill. "Of course. Let me know if the marks spread further or if you feel any other changes."

Changes. He almost laughed at that. Everything was changing. The marks were spreading, his old life was catching up with him, and his feelings for Iris were taking root in his chest at the worst possible time.

"I will," he muttered, already moving toward the curtains. He paused before he pushed them aside, fighting the urge to look back, yank her into his arms, and send all caution spiraling into the ether.

Instead, he parted the heavy fabric, strode through the empty shop, ignored the bell as he tugged open the door, and stepped out into the sleepy village.

Stamping his feet, he proceeded down the sidewalk. Somewhere behind him, a rooster crowed and horses whinnied in the stables. Vaskel cast a glance across the snowy street to the tinker shop, which was still quiet and dark. Maybe that meant Lira and Korl weren't awake yet.

The whiff of yeast and sugar now clung to the icy breeze. At least he knew that Pip Brambleheart was awake and baking, just as he was every morning. A distant splash told him the waterwheel was turning, and a muffled clang signaled the blacksmith was hard at work. Everything was just as it should be in Wayside. Everything but him.

Vaskel pressed a hand to his arm, then gave a rough shake of his head. He couldn't think about the marks or how fast they might be spreading. He could only think about how he had to protect those he loved from the deal he'd made so many years ago, how he was going to keep them safe from Marina.

Even if it meant giving the hellkin exactly what he'd promised her.

Nine

THE SCENT HIT Vaskel before he even reached the bakery door, and his stomach, which had been knotted with worry since leaving Iris's shop, loosened slightly at the familiar aroma. It was impossible to hold tight to dark thoughts when met with the halfling baker's enthusiasm and exceptional pastries.

He pulled open the glass door and a gust of heat and the heady aroma of sweet rolls engulfed him before Pip's head popped up from behind the counter, his hair standing on end and dusted with a startling amount of flour.

"Vaskel!" The halfling's face split into a delighted grin. "My first customer of the day!"

Despite everything, Vaskel felt his lips curve into a smile. Pip's joy was like sunshine breaking through storm clouds. "Morning, Pip. What has you so excited today?"

"What doesn't have me excited?" Pip bounced on his toes, his hands already reaching for the tongs. "I've been up since three working on flavors for Lira's wedding cake. It has to be spectacular, you know. The most magnificent confection Wayside has ever seen!"

"Lira's wedding." The words came out softer than Vaskel intended, as he wondered if he would be around to witness it or if he'd have to flee Wayside to keep his friends safe. He pushed that thought aside. "I've heard about the five tier cake."

"Oh, that's only half of it." Pip leaned forward conspiratorially, lowering his voice even though they were alone in the shop. "I want to surprise her with a distinct flavor for each tier. Speaking of which..." He whirled around and produced a small plate with a delicate slice of cake. "Would you do me the honor of being my taste tester? This is my newest creation—rosewater cake with vanilla buttercream."

Vaskel accepted the fork Pip offered and took a bite. The cake was light as air, the rosewater delicate without being overpowering, and the vanilla buttercream so smooth it melted on his tongue. It was excellent, as everything Pip made was excellent.

"It's very good," he said honestly, setting down the fork. "Elegant."

Pip's eyes narrowed slightly. "But?"

"But if you're asking my preference..." Vaskel shifted from one leg to the other. "I wouldn't crave this cake like I crave your lemon sweet rolls."

The halfling's expression brightened even more. "Lemon!" He smacked his hand against his forehead, leaving a perfect floury handprint. "Of course! Why didn't I think of it before? Lemon cake! It's usually a spring flavor but paired with coconut or even a ribbon of dark chocolate..."

Pip's words trailed off, and then he was whirling around his kitchen like an electrified sprite, pulling down bowls and muttering about lemon curd and coconut ratios. The halfling's excitement was so pure, so utterly removed from the darkness creeping under Vaskel's skin, that for a moment he could almost forget about the marks and the soul bind.

"Here!" Pip thrust a paper bag at him, as if remembering that the hellkin was still there. "Orange spice sweet rolls. My new winter flavor. The same recipe I sent in my last letter to my cousins in Elmshire. They aren't lemon, but they have warming spices, so they're like a cross between cinnamon rolls and lemon ones. Perfect for a snowy day, wouldn't you say?"

Vaskel glanced out the window, surprised to see that snow had indeed begun to fall while he'd been inside.

"How much do I owe you?" Vaskel reached for the coins tucked in a pocket of his vest, but Pip waved him off.

"Nothing! Consider it payment for the cake testing and the lemon inspiration." The halfling had already pivoted back to his workspace and was humming to himself, clearly lost in visions of the perfect wedding cake.

Vaskel tucked the warm bag under his arm, the heat seeping through the paper and working against the chill in his bones that had nothing to do with the weather. "Thank you, Pip."

"Thank you, my friend!" Pip called back, already elbow-deep in a mixing bowl.

Before he made it to the door, a figure bustled in and almost ran straight into him.

"Vaskel?" The elf threw back his fur-lined hood that was flecked with quickly melting snow. He wore emerald green robes lined with white fur and surprisingly practical, knee-high boots. His silver hair was pristine, as always. "What a pleasure to run into you, dear boy."

Vaskel was a bit surprised to see Lira's uncle in the bakery, but since the elf had arrived in Wayside he'd been trying to fit into the community more instead of sending his attendants to do everything for him.

"How are you?" Vaskel asked.

The elf fluttered one bejeweled hand. "Busy with wedding plans, of course, and trying to see how many Elven wedding customs Lira will permit me."

"What are Elven wedding customs?" Vaskel asked, genuinely curious.

Erindil rubbed his slender fingers together. "Oh, they're magnificent! First, there's the binding of souls ceremony at dawn, where the couple exchanges vows in the ancient tongue while standing in a circle of moonflowers. Then the bride and groom put honey on each other's tongues. Honey from a single variety of flower, so it's incredibly delicious. That flower then becomes their flower, to be grown in their garden."

He stopped himself, shaking his head with a rueful smile. "But that's all far too elaborate and fussy for Lira." He adjusted one of his many rings, the blue gem catching the winter light. "I agree, of course. Not to mention the fact that we're far from Lananore. I don't know where I'd get moonflowers here." He sighed and smiled. "So, we're keeping things simple. Just an outdoor ceremony with me escorting her down the aisle and Glen processing with the rings." He snapped his fingers. "That reminds me. I need to talk to Tinpin about fashioning him a special harness. He'll be most upset if he doesn't match the rest of the wedding party."

Vaskel kept his expression neutral, though an ostrich ring bearer in a custom-made harness might not be everyone's idea of simple. "Naturally."

"Tell me," Erindil said, his tone shifting to something more serious as he studied Vaskel with ageless eyes. "Does Lira seem nervous to you? About the wedding, I mean?"

Vaskel considered the question. Lira has seemed on edge lately, but he suspected it was nothing serious. "Just normal bride jitters, I think. She and Korl adore each other. Anyone can see that."

"Yes," Erindil agreed softly. "Love has a way of finding us when we least expect it, doesn't it?"

Vaskel wondered what the elf meant. Erindil had lived for thousands of years, so he'd presumably loved and lost many times before. Part of him wanted to ask the elf how he dealt with loss, but it seemed a dark shift after chatting about wedding plans.

"Well, I'd better get to the tavern before Sass sends out a search party." Vaskel held up the bag of baked goods. "For the sweet rolls. Not me."

Erindil laughed, patting his arm. "Yes, yes. How droll! I'm here to get some of Pip's confections as well. Glen is quite taken with his sweet rolls." The elf's expression became stern. "Now the trick is hiding them so the rest of us can get a bite."

"We also have to do that with Sass."

Erindil threw his head back with laughter as Vaskel bid him farewell and ducked outside and into the falling snow. He pulled out one of the orange spice rolls from the bag. It was still warm, the glaze slightly melted, and when he bit into it, the flavors of citrus and cinnamon burst onto his tongue. He'd told Pip that his favorite sweet rolls were lemon, but these might be a close second. And the halfling had been right. They were perfect for a wintery day.

He continued chewing as he trekked toward The Tusk & Tail Tavern, glimpsing the former barkeep, Durn, sweeping away snow from the front of the chandler's shop across the street, while his gnome wife dusted the lamps in the window. He raised a hand in greeting, which the broad-shouldered man returned.

The snow continued to fall, coating his shoulders and horns, but Vaskel barely noticed as he trudged along toward the stone bridge that led to the castle. Then a loud clang made him jerk to attention and the bakery bag slip from his fingers.

Ten

VASKEL SCOOPED up the bag from the pile of snow it had landed in, the citrus and cinnamon scent now overpowered by the smell of smoke that always hung around the blacksmith's forge. Metal clanged again metal once more, drawing his gaze to the two orcs who stood outside their shop despite the falling snow. They were working on an iron piece so large that Vaskel walked closer to get a better look.

Wrought iron had been twisted and shaped into an arch of

delicate vines and flowers that bloomed and curved, creating a free-standing and four-sided bower that could only be for one purpose.

"That's extraordinary," Vaskel called out as he reached them.

Klaff looked up from where he was holding a section steady, his green face splitting into a pleased grin. "Vaskel! Good to see you."

Vorto, wielding the hammer, paused with the metal tool overhead. "Come to check on our progress? Korl's been fretting we won't have it done in time."

"I had no idea you were building the ceremony arch." He was touched by the obvious care the two orcs were putting into their work. "It's stunning."

"It's been a secret," Klaff said, adjusting his grip on the iron vine he held. "Not that we can keep something this sizable a secret for very long."

Vaskel tipped his head back. "It is large. I suppose it's a good thing Lira and Korl are getting married outside."

Vorto lowered the hammer and put one meaty hand on his hip. "An outdoor wedding in the winter? I keep asking how that's going to work."

Vaskel chuckled. "Elf magic, from what I understand. Lira always envisioned an outdoor wedding, but neither she nor Korl wanted to wait until spring, so Erindil is pulling off the same enchantment that keeps his camp so warm, but on a bigger scale."

Klaff grunted. "Elf magic, eh? Do you think that's why Lira's baking is so good?"

Vorto shot his partner a look. "If that was the case, Lira's gran must have been an elf because she could bake up a storm." He held up a finger. "And we know she wasn't."

"Neither is Pip, but no one makes sweet rolls like he does." Vaskel held up the paper bag. "Speaking of sweet rolls, I've got Pip's new orange spice version. Care to try them?"

Both orcs' eyes lit up as they carefully lowered the iron structure and dropped their tools.

"Orange spice?" Vorto accepted a roll with reverence. "What will that little baker think of next?"

As the two orcs ate their rolls and mumbled sugary thanks, Vaskel stepped closer to the arch to study the intricate metalwork more closely. The blooms fashioned from metal looked as real as the small birds perched on the curving branches.

"It's more than beautiful," Vaskel said, stepping back. "It's art."

Klaff beamed, orange glaze dribbling down his chin. "You hear that, Vort? Art, he says."

"Don't let it go to your head," Vorto rumbled, but he was smiling too. "Though I'll admit, we're rather proud of this one."

Klaff brushed his sticky hands on his pants and tipped his head to the arch. "Mind giving us a hand? It will be easier with three sets of hands."

Vaskel didn't hesitate, setting down the bag of rolls and moving to support the iron where Klaff pointed. The metal was cold under his palms, but there was something grounding about the work that helped him forget about his worries.

"So," Vorto said, as he began hammering a metal branch, "you know much about orc wedding traditions?"

Vaskel shook his head, keeping the arch steady as the two orcs worked. "Can't say I do."

Klaff struck a steam beam with his hammer, and it vibrated through the entire arch. "Traditionally, the bride or groom carries a boulder down the aisle."

"A boulder?" Vaskel couldn't hide his amusement at the thought of Lira hefting a rock. The half-elf was tough, but rogue work had never demanded she heft boulders.

"The groom—or other groom—" Vorto said.

"Or other bride," Klaff interrupted.

Vorto inclined his head to his partner. "Or other bride has to carry one too. Then they break them together with hammers to show they can overcome any obstacle."

"Somehow I don't see that fitting Lira and Korl's ceremony," Vaskel said, drawing grins from the orcs.

"No," Klaff agreed, swiping a hand across his brow. "It's not Korl's style either."

"Then there's the feast." Vorto's dark eyes glittered. "Seven courses, each one spicier than the last. By the end, even orcs are sweating."

"And the wrestling match," Klaff added. "The couple wrestles as a team, and it's considered an honor to challenge them."

Vaskel grinned and shook his head, trying to picture Lira in a wrestling match. "I think Erindil would be scandalized."

Korl's dads continued sharing increasingly outlandish orc wedding traditions—some Vaskel was certain they were making up—while they worked on the arch.

"Of course," Klaff said as he straightened and appraised their work, "Lira's not an orc, so we can hardly expect her to follow our traditions. But she's family now, orc or not."

"You couldn't have asked for a better addition to your family," Vaskel said.

Vorto nodded with enthusiasm. "She understands him and lets him be himself. Not everyone would."

Vaskel's throat was suddenly tight. Lira had always accepted others for who they were, probably because she hadn't felt she fit in for so long. It was why she'd never looked at him differently despite his infernal nature, and it was one of the many things he admired about his friend.

The thought of Marina touching any of this, any of them, made his hands clench on the iron and his knuckles go white beneath the crimson flesh.

"Steady there," Klaff said gently, noticing his grip had tightened.

"Sorry." Vaskel loosened his hold, pushing down the dark thoughts.

Vorto eyed him. "You have something on your mind, son?"

Before he could assure them he was fine, Klaff flapped a hand. "We've kept you too long, haven't we? They're probably waiting for you at the Tusk & Tail."

Vaskel summoned a grin, grateful for the easy excuse. "I suppose I should get to work."

Vorto winked. "You don't want Sass coming to look for you. Especially if she's expecting those sweet rolls."

Vaskel laughed. "You're right."

"Never get between a dwarf and their food," Klaff said, as if reciting a solemn oath.

Vaskel plucked the pastry bag from the ground, glad there were still sweet rolls to offer Sass. "Good advice."

Klaff held Vaskel's gaze for a beat. "You ever need more, we're here."

Vaskel nodded as he resumed his walk to the tavern, glancing back at the orcs and wondering if there had been deeper meaning beneath Klaff's words.

Eleven

VASKEL HAD BARELY TAKEN two steps inside the tavern when Lira emerged from the kitchen, loose strands of auburn hair sagging over her eyes and her cheeks flushed. Her brown work dress and the apron tied around it looked like they'd gone a few rounds with a sack of flour and lost dismally.

She held up a finger. "Don't say a word."

Vaskel mimed buttoning his lips, as Sass sauntered across the room from where she'd been straightening chairs.

"Does this have anything to do with a new recipe?" The dwarf asked.

"How hard can it be to create a recipe?" Lira's shoulders sagged. "My gran came up with her own recipes. I should be able to create one that doesn't make Crumpet gag."

Sass pressed her lips together for a beat, clearly stifling a laugh. "Is that wee beastie turning his nose up at your baked goods?"

Lira sniffed, twitching one shoulder. "He's right. The ratios were all wrong, and the cookies were so dry it was like having all the moisture sucked from your mouth as you chewed."

Sass crinkled her brown nose but walked to Lira and led her to a table. "You're being too hard on yourself. No one said you needed to create new recipes. The ones we have work just fine."

"I suppose so," Lira muttered as she sank into a wooden chair.

Vaskel held up his crumpled paper bag. "I've got sweet rolls from Pip, if that helps."

Lira's expression softened slightly. "That helps, especially since I have nothing good to serve you."

Sass took the bag and peered inside. "Two? You only got two?"

Vaskel didn't meet her gaze. "I might have been waylaid by some folks."

Sass held up a hand. "I do not want to hear that someone else ate sweet rolls intended for my belly." She inhaled deeply. "Do I smell orange?"

"They're orange spice sweet rolls," Vaskel said. "Pip's new creation."

Lira slumped over, folding her arms on the table and resting her head on them. "See? Pip can create new recipes, and I'll bet they're perfect."

Sass wasn't able to reply because her mouth was already filled with orange, yeasty goodness, so she attempted to frown and shake her head. Finally, she managed, "'Orrible."

Lira narrowed her eyes, sitting up and snatching the last

remaining roll from the bag. She took a bite and her eyes fluttered shut as she moaned. "They're amazing. If I wasn't marrying Korl, I'd marry these." Then she heaved out a frustrated sigh and stomped back toward the kitchen, the half-doors swinging violently in her wake.

Sass caught Vaskel's eye as she swallowed the rest of her roll and lowered her voice. "Why obsess over creating a new recipe now?"

Vaskel understood all too well the urge to control what you could when bigger things felt overwhelming. "I'll talk to her."

Sass licked the sugary glaze off her fingers. "Good luck to you."

When Vaskel pushed through the swinging doors, he found more flour covering more surfaces and Crumpet and his raccoon friend forming an assembly line to move sad, pale cookies from the baking pan into the trash.

"Want to talk about it?" Vaskel asked, sliding a three-legged stool up to the massive central worktable.

"What's there to talk about?" She didn't meet his eyes. "Baking is supposed to be what calms me, but it can't even do that anymore."

"Is this really about baking?" Vaskel said lightly. "Come on, Lira. What's really bothering you?"

She was quiet for a long moment, absently brushing flour from her apron. "What if it's a mistake?"

"The cookies?" Vaskel teased. "I think those were definitely a mistake."

That earned him a dishtowel tossed in his direction, which he snagged deftly from the air. Crumpet chittered, hurling a loose cookie crumb at him. The winged creature might not have liked the cookies, but he was still defensive of Lira.

"Not the awful cookies." Lira leaned against the table and crossed her arms over her chest. "The wedding."

"You think marrying Korl is a mistake?" Vaskel's eyebrows rose. "The orc who rebuilt your oven, fixed your roof, and looks at you like you hung the moon and stars?"

A smile tugged at the corners of Lira's mouth. "When you put it like that..."

"Lira." He leaned forward, his voice gentling. "Tell me one thing. When you think about waking up next to Korl every morning for the rest of your life, how do you feel?"

A satisfied sigh escaped her lips despite herself. "Safe. Happy. Like I'm exactly where I'm supposed to be."

"Then what's the problem? The runaway wedding? The gnome haberdasher who's nominated himself wedding planner?"

"Yes, no, oh, I don't know." She threw her hands up, and loose flour sifted down onto her hair. "All the wedding fuss has reminded me that this is a big deal, and a permanent one. After years of running with our crew, never staying in one place, never letting anyone get too close..."

"You're scared," Vaskel said simply.

"Terrified," she admitted.

He laughed, surprising her. "Good. If you weren't scared about such a big life change, I'd be worried. But Lira, I've watched you face down wraiths, negotiate with goblins, and build a life here from nothing. You can handle being happy."

She rubbed her arms, as if the kitchen wasn't overly warm from the oven. "Sometimes I'm not sure I deserve this much happiness."

Vaskel felt that right in his gut. "I get that. I do. But if anyone has earned a happily ever after, it's you. You came back to your home, you faced the pain of rebuilding a life without the person who'd made Wayside so special, and you made this town a place that even your wayward friends could call home."

Her eyes shone as she smiled at him.

"Besides," his lips curved into his trademark devilish grin, "even I like Korl, and you know how selective I am about people."

Lira was startled into a laugh. "You've usually been jealous of any guy who showed an interest in me."

"I have not!" He pressed a hand to his chest in mock offense, then laughed when she gave him a knowing look. "All right, perhaps a little. But only because none of them were good enough for you."

"And Korl is?"

"Korl is. He's steady where you're impulsive, quiet where you're chatty, and he adores you completely." He cocked his head at her. "You know, you were one of the few females who could ever resist me. My devastating charms just rolled right off you."

"That's because we're such good friends," Lira said softly. "Real friends."

Something in Vaskel's chest squeezed at her words. They *were* friends, true friends, and here she was trusting him with her fears while he kept his own locked away.

The marks on his arm prickled, reminding him of their presence, of Marina's presence, of the danger he might bring to Lira's door. He wanted to tell her, wanted to warn her, but he couldn't add to her burden. Not now.

"But you were tempted by me, weren't you?" He shot her a sultry smile. "Admit it."

She laughed, shaking her head. "I'm sorry, Vask. I never saw you as anything but a friend."

He mimed being pierced by an arrow in his heart, but Lira swatted at him with another dishtowel. "As if you cared. You had every other female swooning at your feet."

He chuckled, not wanting to admit that all those swooning females had meant nothing. Hellkins might have a talent for seduction, but he craved something deeper now. Something real. Something like Lira had with Korl.

"Then I suppose I'll have to forget about my plans to object at your wedding."

Lira barked a laugh. "You'd never!"

"Of course not." He winked at her. "I know better than to anger an orc—or three of them."

"Not that your objections would make the wedding less

dramatic with Erindil involved." Lira shook her head, and he wondered if she knew about her ostrich ring bearer yet.

Before he could tell her, loud chattering broke the moment, and they both turned to see Crumpet on the counter, gesticulating wildly at the stove where a pot of chai was bubbling over, sending spiced milk cascading onto the stovetop with an angry hiss.

"Son of a wand waxer!" Lira rushed to rescue the pot while Crumpet flew to perch on the copper pots overhead and the raccoon ambled to the windowsill.

When the pot was off the heat, Vaskel picked up an earthenware mug from a shelf and held it to Lira. "Since the chai is ready..."

Twelve

THE FAMILIAR RHYTHM of tending bar should have been soothing. Pour ale, wipe counter, exchange pleasantries with regulars, repeat. But tonight, Vaskel flicked his gaze to the door every few minutes, his tail twitching with barely concealed anxiety. Each time the hinges creaked, his head snapped up, hoping to see Iris sweep through in a swirl of jingling skirts.

But she hadn't come.

"Another ale, Vask?" Old Henrik, the village cooper, raised his empty tankard.

"Coming right up." Vaskel forced his trademark grin as he pulled a pint. "How's the barrel business?"

"Can't complain. Though Pip ordered three new ones for storage. Says he's planning something special for the wedding." Henrik's weathered face creased. "You know what he's cooking up?"

"Besides himself into a frenzy?" Vaskel chuckled, thinking of the frenzied baker testing out cake flavors that morning. "Whatever Pip creates, it'll be spectacular."

Henrik laughed, returning to his conversation with the miller at the next table. Vaskel's smile faded the moment the old man looked away. Where was Iris? She'd promised to scour her books to find a solution. Her absence could only mean she'd found nothing. Or worse, that what she'd found was too terrible to share.

The door burst open with enough force to make everyone look up, and Thrain stumbled in with Rog at his side, both of them pink-cheeked and laughing.

"Vaskel!" Thrain boomed, weaving only slightly as he made his way to the bar, his heavy greatcoat flapping around his legs. "My friend! My very dear, very red friend!"

"How much of Rosie's brandy have you had?" Vaskel asked, though he couldn't help but smile at the dwarf's exuberance.

Thrain stroked a hand down his dark beard, scrunching his mouth as he pondered the question.

"Not nearly as much as that ostrich had during the Solstice Festival!" Rog clambered onto a stool with more difficulty than usual, his blue beard barely poking above the bar top.

The two dissolved into laughter again, and despite everything, Vaskel felt his spirits lift. There was something infectious about their good mood, something pure and uncomplicated that he desperately needed tonight.

The other patrons were watching now, smiling at the pair's antics. This was what Vaskel loved about the Tusk & Tail, about

Wayside itself. The way joy spread like ripples on water, touching everyone it reached.

"You know what the best part is?" Rog said, suddenly becoming serious in that way only the inebriated could manage. "That silly bird might have caused a lot of trouble, but he also gave us an adventure." The gnome slapped his palm on the bar. "I'd been missing our adventures."

"To adventures!" Thrain raised an imaginary glass. "And to Glen."

"To Glen!" several patrons echoed, raising their actual drinks.

Vaskel pulled two ales and slid them across the bar to his tipsy friends. "On the house, for the entertainment."

"You're a prince among hellkins," Thrain declared, then paused. "Are there hellkin princes? Is that a thing?"

Before Vaskel could answer, the kitchen door swung open and Lira emerged, carrying a tray of something that smelled absolutely divine. She'd clearly recovered from her morning's baking disaster. Her apron was fresh, her hair neatly braided, and her smile warm.

"Fresh from the oven," she announced, setting the tray on the bar. "Cranberry scones, thanks to our new woodland supplier."

"The raccoon?" whispered Vaskel, not sure if it was supposed to be common knowledge that Lira's baking assistants were animals.

"I've named him Bramble, since he brings me lots of bramble berries from the forest."

Vaskel searched his mind to remember what berries grew in the forest, wondering if the new kitchen assistant might pilfer from other kitchens. Regardless, the cranberry scones smelled divine. They were golden brown, studded with bright red berries, and topped with large granules of sugar. Vaskel's mouth watered just looking at them.

"For me?" Thrain reached for one, but Lira playfully slapped his hand away.

"The first one goes to Vaskel," she said, picking up the most perfect scone and offering it to him. "A thank you for earlier. For listening. For being such a good friend."

He accepted the scone with a small bow. "No thank you required, but the scone is very appreciated."

"Now you can have one," Lira told Thrain, who immediately grabbed two and passed one to Rog.

"Remember that time we found that enchanted bakery in the Whispering Woods?" Rog said through a mouthful of scone. "Everything tasted like your favorite childhood memory,"

"I remember we barely escaped." Lira narrowed her gaze at her former crew mate. "I remember Cali shooting us out of there while you begged to be left with the cream cakes."

Rog's gaze didn't meet hers. "Don't remember that bit."

"These are better than cream cakes," Thrain declared, even though he hadn't been with them when they'd stumbled upon the enchanted bakery or the deceptively delectable cakes.

Crumbles scattered the gnome's beard. "I won't argue with you. 'Specially since I don't remember why we're arguing."

Thrain slapped his leg and roared with laughter. Vaskel rolled his eyes, biting into his own scone and savoring the tart burst of berry melding perfectly with the butteriness.

Lira shook her head and left the tray of scones next to Vaskel. "Make sure those two eat another to soak up whatever they've been drinking."

Vaskel eyed the scones then the dwarf and gnome crying tears of laughter. "It might take more scones than we have."

Lira winked at him as she turned on her heel. "There are always more scones."

For a moment, Vaskel let himself get lost in the sweetness of the scones and the safety of the tavern. For a moment, he let himself believe that nothing was wrong.

Thirteen

SHE HADN'T COME. He'd waited all night for Iris, but she'd never come. As much as he wanted to believe it was because she'd been so busy working on a cure, he suspected the news was worse. What if she hadn't come because she didn't want to give him the bad news? What if she couldn't bear to tell him there was nothing she could do, no way she could save him?

As Vaskel stepped from the tavern and into the night, the village was silent save for the whisper of falling snow. Heading toward the inn, his shoulders hunched against the cold as his boots crunched the snow. The marks on his arms itched, and he scratched at them through his shirt and cloak. They'd reached his shoulder now, and soon they'd be visible to everyone, no matter how high he pulled his collar.

He picked up his pace, eager to escape the cold and find solace in his room at the inn. Then he took a quick breath, catching the scent of something both familiar and long forgotten. It was faint enough to vanish on the breeze, but not before certainty settled in his gut.

Vaskel's steps slowed, his tail going rigid as wariness slithered down his spine. He'd survived too many ambushes, too many supposedly safe nights that had turned deadly, to ignore the prickling sensation at the back of his neck. His skill at detecting danger had been why he'd bound his soul to Marina in the first place.

His hand drifted to where a blade would have been back in his adventuring days, and he cursed himself for not taking precautions.

"Hello, Vaskel."

The voice slid from the shadows beside the bakery, as smooth as well-aged whiskey and twice as intoxicating. A voice he hadn't heard in years but would recognize anywhere, in any lifetime.

Marina stepped into the moonlight, and his breath caught in his throat.

She hadn't aged a day. Her skin was the deep crimson of fresh blood, darker than his own, and it seemed to glow against the falling snow. Her hair spilled in waves of black past her shoulders, and those devastating amber eyes that had once made him do terrible, foolish things glinted as if lit from within. She wore black leather that clung to every dangerous curve, and her tail swayed behind her hypnotically.

He sucked in a sharp breath, the smoky, sultry scent of her now filling his nostrils and dredging up memories that slammed into him.

"Marina." The name scraped past his lips like a curse.

Her laugh was low and rich, the sound wrapping around him like silk bindings. "You look startled to see me, my darling. I would think you'd be expecting me."

She moved closer, and he found himself frozen, unable to retreat or advance. The marks on his skin seared in response to her proximity, pulsing with a heat that had everything to do with the bond between them. "Just because I was expecting you doesn't mean I wasn't dreading you."

She hummed in response, cocking her head to one side as she studied him. She finally reached out to trace a finger along his jaw. "You look weary. This quaint little village life doesn't suit you. You're meant for more than pouring ale and pretending to be tame."

He flinched but didn't pull away. He couldn't. "I'm not pretending anything," he managed, though his voice came out more ragged than intended.

"No?" Her hand slid down to rest over his heart, which thrummed restlessly. "Then why does our bond burn? Why does your heart pound for me?"

"That's not—" He stopped, unable to deny what they both knew was true. The soul bind wasn't just spreading. The embers scorching his veins were pulling him toward her with every beat of his heart.

"I've come to collect what's mine," Marina said simply, as if discussing the weather. "Our deal, remember? Your soul bound to mine for eternity. You can't run from it, Vaskel. You can't hide from it in this sleepy village."

"I'm not hiding. This is my home now."

She laughed again, but there was an edge to it this time. "Home? These simple villagers with their simple lives? You're a hellkin, Vaskel. You're meant for chaos and passion, for danger and debauchery." She gestured dismissively at the peaceful village around them. "Not this."

"You know nothing about my life here."

"I know enough." Her eyes glowed brighter, and the marks on his skin responded, sending flames licking up his arm. "I know you tend bar like a common servant. I know you pine for that human apothecary who'll never understand your true nature. I know you pretend to be satisfied with friendship and belonging when your blood sings for more."

Each word was a dagger, perfectly aimed.

"I have a new crew," Marina continued, stepping so close he could breathe in her scent of smoldering ash and dark promises. "Hellkins who understand what we are and what we're meant to be. No more hiding, no more pretending. Just power and freedom and the life you were born to live."

She reached up, her fingers tangling in his hair, pulling his head down until their faces were inches apart. "Come with me, Vaskel. Leave this place behind. Be who you were always meant to be."

The soul bind pulled at him, demanding, insisting, screaming that he belonged with her, to her, that this was his fate. Marina smiled, knowing she had him. Knowing the bind would win.

"I've waited long enough to collect," she purred, her breath warm against his lips. "It's time, Vaskel."

Fourteen

VASKEL STARED DOWN AT MARINA, waiting for the familiar pull of desire, the heat that had once consumed him whenever she was near. He waited for his blood to sing, for his resolve to crumble, and for all the old hungers to resurface.

Nothing came.

Where once there had been an inferno, now there was only ash. Where once her beauty had devastated him, now he saw it for what it was. It was a weapon, as cold as the most sharply forged steel.

The soul bind might burn in his veins, but his heart remained unmoved.

"No." The word came out steady and certain.

Marina's perfectly sculpted eyebrows rose. "No?"

"I'm happy here, Marina. Genuinely happy." He stepped back, breaking her hold on him. "I have friends who accept me for who I am, not what I can do for them. I have work that matters and a life I've chosen rather than one that was cobbled together from what was stolen from others."

Her eyes narrowed, but her smile never wavered. "You've gone soft."

"I've grown up." He straightened his shoulders, meeting her gaze without flinching. "I'm not the hellkin you used to know. That version of me who was reckless, hungry for chaos, and willing to bind his soul for power doesn't exist anymore."

Marina circled him slowly, her tail slashing. The snow continued to fall around them, catching in her midnight hair, melting against her crimson skin. She moved with the same lethal grace she always had, but now Vaskel saw the calculation in it, the performance.

"A reformed hellkin," she purred, stopping in front of him again. "This newfound nobility suits you. It makes you more fascinating."

"I'm not interested in being fascinating to you."

"Don't tell me you haven't missed me, darling, because I've missed you." Her voice cracked, as if the truth had broken its way through the cunning facade. "We were alike, you and me. We understood each other. I haven't found anyone who's truly understood me since you."

Was the hellkin lonely? Vaskel had never imagined her capable of such a human emotion. Not that it mattered. He wasn't the same hellkin he'd been, and if he'd ever understood her, he didn't now.

"I'm not like you anymore, Marina. I took a different path once you left. I chose a different life."

Her expression hardened and her laugh was ice. "Oh, Vaskel. You think you have a choice about this? The soul bind isn't some trivial enchantment you can shrug off because you've developed a conscience. It's eternal."

"But not unbreakable."

"You think the village apothecary will break it?" Marina's eyes flashed malice, and the marks on his skin flared in response, sending spikes of pain up his arms. "How sweet. You really have gone native, haven't you?"

She stepped closer again, and this time her expression had shifted from seductive to dangerous. "Let me be very clear, my darling. You can play house in this quaint little village for now, but eventually, the bind will call you back to me. And when you resist —because I know you will resist—the pain will become unbearable."

"I can handle pain."

"Can your friends?" The question hung in the frosty air between them. "My new crew of young hellkins is eager to prove themselves and to earn their place at my side. If I told them there was a village harboring a contract breaker, a hellkin who'd broken his sacred oath..." She trailed off, letting the implications settle like the gathering snow.

Vaskel's hands curled into fists. "You wouldn't."

"Wouldn't I?" She tilted her head, studying him with those burning eyes. "Your little baker friend—Lira, isn't it? And that dwarf from the Ice Lands. The orc guard and his fathers. The halfling brothers and their fussy gnome friend." She counted them off on her fingers like a shopping list. "So many soft targets. So many ways for things to go wrong."

"If you touch them—"

"You'll what?" Marina interrupted, her voice amused. "Fight me? Break the bind? You can't, and we both know it. The only way to keep them safe is to honor our deal. Come with me willingly, and this peaceful little village remains peaceful."

She reached up, her hand cupping his cheek with mock tenderness. "Think about it, darling. But don't think too long. My patience isn't infinite, and my crew grows restless."

She rose onto her toes and pressed her lips to his cheek. The kiss burned like frostbite.

"I'll give you three days," she whispered against his ear. "Three days to say your goodbyes, to get your affairs in order. Then you come to me, or I come for them."

He clenched his teeth so hard he could hear them grinding.

For the briefest flash, he thought he caught genuine affection flickering across her face. "You always looked magnificent when you were trying to be noble, Vaskel. It's almost enough to make me genuinely fond of you again."

She pulled away, already melting back into the shadows between the buildings. Her form seemed to dissolve into the swirling snow, but her voice drifted back to him like smoke.

"It will be just like it always was between us, darling. I'll have you and you'll have me. Soon enough, you'll forget all about this village and these people."

Then she was gone, leaving only the faint scent of brimstone and the phantom burn of her icy kiss on his cheek.

Vaskel stood alone in the falling snow, his body trembling and the marks on his arms pulsing. Each pulse was a reminder of the bond, of the deal he'd made so long ago when he'd been young and stupid and thought powers were worth any price.

Dread settled cold and heavy in his stomach. Marina never made idle threats. If he didn't go with her, she would bring her crew here. They would burn the Tusk & Tail to the ground. They would hurt everyone he cared about, and Marina would make him watch.

Three days. Three days to break an unbreakable bond, or three days to say goodbye to the only real home he'd ever known.

He pressed a hand to his arm and the scorching marks. He believed Marina that the pain would become unbearable. But that wasn't what terrified him.

What terrified him was the thought of Marina's new crew descending on Wayside like crimson locusts, destroying everything beautiful and good.

The snow continued to drift down, the wet flakes covering Marina's footprints as if she'd never been there. But the marks on his skin throbbed with every beat of his heart, counting down until he lost Wayside or Wayside lost everything.

Fifteen

VASKEL PAUSED outside the apothecary the next morning, glancing first one way and then the other. No one else was walking around in the faint dawn light, and not even the scent of yeast and sugar from Pip's bakery laced the breeze. The hellkin knew it was too early to be pestering Iris, but he'd already been up for hours and he could wait no longer.

Sleep had been impossible. Between the marks spreading like dragon fire across his skin and Marina's threats echoing in his mind, Vaskel had spent the night staring at the ceiling of his small room at the inn, counting down the hours until the sun broke through the darkness. He absently touched the hilt of the blade he'd tucked into his belt and then scraped at his arm before he slowly tested the door. Releasing a breath when the handle gave way, the hellkin opened the door slow enough that he could catch the bell overhead before it jangled.

Once he was inside, he was consumed by the silence of the dark shop. For a moment, the silence stretched, and worry crept up his spine. He'd assumed that Iris had left the door open for him, but maybe he'd been wrong. Had she forgotten to lock up? Had something happened? Had Marina—?

The heavy curtain leading to the back room flew aside, and Iris's head popped out, her face splitting into a grin. "Oh, good! I hoped it was you. Anyone else, and I was going to have a lot of explaining to do."

The curtain dropped back into place, then her head appeared again almost immediately. "Come on in and lock the door behind you. We don't want any surprise visitors."

He clicked the bolt into place with a definitive snap, then made his way around the counter and pushed through the heavy velvet into Iris's private domain.

Although shadows had shrouded the front of the shop, the back room glowed from lit lanterns and flickering candles. The bookwyrms were in full flutter overhead, their iridescent wings catching the lamplight as they darted between the towering shelves. But it was the state of the room that gave him pause. Books lay open on every available surface—the round table, the chairs, even stacked on the floor in precarious towers. Half-drunk cups of tea perched on the edge of the table, balanced on top of open tomes, and one teetered dangerously on the arm of an overstuffed chair.

"Have you been working on this all night?" he asked, picking his way carefully around the books.

She nodded, pushing a wayward curl behind her ear only for it to spring free immediately. "What else would I be doing? We might not have much time."

Vaskel swallowed hard, the marks pulsing beneath his shirt. She didn't know how right she was. "Iris, I need to tell you something."

She looked up from the massive tome she'd been studying, her green eyes sharp despite the exhaustion etched into her features. "What is it?"

"Marina found me. Last night, after I left the tavern." The words tumbled out. "She's alive, and she's given me three days— well, a little over two days now—to honor our soul bind and join her new crew. If I don't..." He couldn't finish the sentence, couldn't voice the threat against everyone he loved.

Iris listened without interrupting, her brow furrowing and her half-moon glasses sliding down her nose. When his words drifted off, she nodded resolutely as if his news changed nothing. "Like I said, not much time."

Vaskel squared his shoulders, encouraged because the woman's determination to help him hadn't wavered.

She turned back to the books, gesturing for him to join her. "I've found several possibilities. Some are more extreme than others, but desperate times and all that."

They bent over the ancient texts together, shoulders nearly touching as they read. Iris explained each potential remedy she'd found—a cleansing ritual that required moonwater and fur from an extinct species, a counter-curse that might break the bond but would probably kill them both, and a potion made from ingredients so rare they might as well be mythical.

Vaskel found it increasingly difficult to concentrate. This close to the apothecary, he could see the way she bit her lower lip when she was thinking hard. An errant curl had escaped again, falling across her face as she read, and his fingers itched to brush it back, to tangle in those dark waves and—

"Vaskel?"

He blinked. Furrows bunched her brow, and he realized she'd been saying his name.

"Vaskel, are you all right?"

He snapped back to attention, heat crawling up his neck that had nothing to do with the soul bind. "Sorry, my mind wandered."

Iris studied him for a moment, and something in her expression softened. "Don't worry," she breathed. "We'll figure this out. We have to."

She placed her hand over his where it rested on the table, and the simple touch sent a jolt through him that made the soul bind's burning seem like nothing more than a sunbeam. Her hand was soft and warm and steady, and it brought to mind the feeling of coming home after a long, dangerous quest. It was safety and belonging and everything he'd been searching for without knowing it.

This was torture of an entirely different kind than what Marina had inflicted. The soul bind might consume him, but being this close to Iris, feeling her touch and knowing he couldn't act on these feelings—not now, not with Marina's threat hanging over them, not when pursuing anything with Iris might paint an even bigger target on her back—*that* might destroy him faster than any curse ever could.

He cleared his throat and summoned a smile. "I know we will. I have you on my side, don't I?"

"A friend is someone who knows your faults and still loves you." She squeezed his hand. "I will always be your friend, Vaskel, and I will always be on your side."

Sixteen

BRIGHT LIGHT FILTERED through the skylight, falling across Vaskel's face and rousing him from an uncomfortable sleep. His neck protested violently as he straightened in the overstuffed armchair, every vertebra seeming to crack in sequence. Books lay scattered around him, and a bookwyrm slept coiled on the arm of the chair, tiny iridescent wings draped across his scaled green snout.

Iris was nowhere to be seen, probably catching a few hours of proper sleep in her rooms above the shop. They'd reviewed every ritual or spell that seemed even remotely workable, but finally their heavy eyelids and unstifled yawns had been enough of a distraction that he'd slumped into the chair to rest his eyes while Iris had made drowsy sounds about brewing more tea.

Vaskel stretched, careful not to disturb the bookwyrm on the chair or the others snoozing on top of open books or in the wells of saucers. It was officially morning now, which meant he needed to head to the tavern even if he was still short a decent night's sleep.

With a glance toward the back of the building and the staircase that wound upstairs to Iris's quarters, he decided not to bother Iris. She deserved to sleep after staying up all night searching for a way to save him. He only wished they'd found anything to give him hope.

Vaskel made his way through the curtain and the shop, careful to hold the bell overhead and dampen any telltale jingling. Once he was outside, the hellkin blinked in the morning light bouncing off the snow. He glanced around quickly, checking if anyone had seen him emerge from the apothecary, but all the business of the village seemed to happen at the town square. Besides, there was nothing unusual about him popping into the apothecary. Considering the number of powders and elixirs he'd bought since he'd been in Wayside, some might argue it would be more unusual if he wasn't there.

Still, he walked carefully away, his tail snapping in alarm when the door to the haberdashery next door flew open.

"Vaskel! Is that you?" Tinpin's head popped out, his pointed hat slightly askew. "I'm delighted to see you. Just delighted!"

"Morning, Tin," Vaskel managed, trying to edge away. "I was just—"

"Perfect timing! Perfect!" The gnome hurried outside and grabbed his arm with surprising strength and pulled him toward the shop. "You need to be fitted for the wedding. Lira and Korl were very specific about the wedding party's attire. Very specific!

Or was it Erindil who was specific?" He flapped a hand in the air. "No matter, no matter."

"I really should—" Vaskel tried to protest, acutely aware that his marks would be hard to hide during a fitting.

"It won't take a minute!" the gnome insisted, already dragging him through the door. "Not a minute!"

The haberdashery smelled of wool and lavender, with bolts of colorful fabric propped along the walls. Buttons gleamed from glass jars like jewels, and ribbons cascaded from hooks.

"Back here, back here!" Tinpin gestured to a small platform at the back of the shop. "Arms out, that's it!"

The gnome produced a measuring tape from his brown tweed vest, chattering continuously as he measured. "You're going to look absolutely splendid in the claret-colored velvet that Lira and Korl selected. Splendid! Some might say not to put red on red, but I think they're wrong. Dead wrong. Besides, these are two distinct shades and your skin has more purple undertones."

Vaskel stood still, letting the gnome's patter wash over him. He desperately hoped he would be there for the wedding.

"I'm thinking," Tinpin tapped his chin with one finger, studying Vaskel with an artist's eye, "an ivory ascot might be just the thing. Yes, indeed. Yes, indeed. It would provide such lovely contrast. Don't you agree?"

"Sounds perfect," Vaskel agreed automatically, his mind bouncing between Marina's cold threats and Iris's warm smile as she'd assured him they would find a solution.

"And the waistcoat will be a work of art. An absolute work of art." Tinpin continued measuring, jotting notes on a small pad that materialized from another pocket. "Though I do hope I have enough fabric for Klaff and Vorto. Those orcs are substantially larger than I expected. Substantially!"

The gnome's cheerful fretting continued as he finished his measurements, but Vaskel barely heard him. Would he be here for the wedding? Would he stand with Korl as Lira walked down the aisle? Would he raise a toast to the happy couple, dance at their reception, help Sass clean up the tavern afterward while complaining good-naturedly about drunken guests?

Or would he be with Marina's crew, bound forever to a life he no longer wanted?

"All done! All done!" Tinpin announced, stepping back with satisfaction. "You can step down now. The suit will be ready in plenty of time for the ceremony. Plenty of time!"

Vaskel thanked the gnome and extracted himself from the shop, grateful that Tin hadn't requested he disrobe. The fewer who knew about his predicament, the better, even if he felt wretched keeping such a secret from his friends.

There was no way to avoid deception, he told himself as he drew in a breath of cold air. The less the villagers knew, the safer they would be.

As Vaskel turned to continue his trek toward the tavern, the sound of marketplace chatter drew his attention. It wasn't the typical clatter of vendors setting up their stalls for the day's trade that snatched his attention. It was one voice among the merry din that made every hair on the back of his neck stand on end.

That laugh. He stiffened as he turned, instinct telling him he knew the throaty sound designed to charm and entice. He moved closer, his heart hammering against his ribs.

Wooden stalls with faded fabric awnings huddled together, their canvas tops dusted with a fine layer of snow. The air was thick with woodsmoke from the braziers vendors used to keep warm and the earthy richness of root vegetables piled high in woven baskets.

There, at a vegetable stall, stood Marina. But not as he'd last seen her, all leather and danger. Now she wore a simple wool dress in muted brown, her hair braided modestly, looking for all the world like any other village woman doing her morning shopping.

She chatted with the merchant, laughing at something he said, her hand resting lightly on his arm in a gesture that seemed friendly but that Vaskel knew was calculated to the last degree. The merchant, a graying human with all the personality of stale bread, was practically glowing under her attention.

Vaskel's hands clenched into fists, the marks on his arms flaring with heat. She'd promised him three days, although now that he thought back, she hadn't promised she would stay away until the end of them. How like the hellkin to taunt her victim before exacting penance.

His tail swished behind him. "Not on my watch."

Seventeen

VASKEL KEPT to the edges of the market, using the crowd as cover while he tracked Marina's movements. She glided between the stalls like silk across soft skin, admiring a display of winter apples and exclaiming over the quality of speckled duck eggs a farmer's wife had brought to sell. To anyone watching, she appeared to be nothing more than a newcomer to the village, perhaps visiting relatives or passing through on the way to somewhere else.

But Vaskel knew better. He watched the calculated way she

tilted her head when the honey vendor explained his different varieties, saw how her fingers lingered just a moment too long when the elderly herb seller handed her a sprig of rosemary to smell. Each gesture was designed to disarm, to charm, to make herself memorable in the most pleasant way possible.

At the root vegetable stand, she engaged the usually grumpy farmer in an animated conversation about the best way to store turnips through the winter. The man was actually smiling, his weathered face creasing and his cheeks coloring as Marina hung on his every word.

She moved on to admire the fruits at another stall, where preserved quinces and late pears mingled in baskets. The vendor, a middle-aged woman with work-worn hands, initially regarded Marina with the suspicion rural folk reserved for beautiful strangers. But within moments, Marina had her laughing, the two of them bent together over a basket of dried figs as if they were old friends sharing gossip.

This was what made Marina dangerous. It wasn't only her beauty, though that was weapon enough, but it was her ability to read people instantly and become exactly what they wanted her to be. With the men who grinned haplessly at her, she played the innocent, asking their advice and flattering them for being so clever. With some of the women, she was conspiratorial and warm, complimenting their goods and asking after recipes with the eagerness of someone genuinely wanting to learn. With other women, she fluttered her lashes and touched their arms until they blushed.

Vaskel's marks burned beneath his shirt as he watched her work. She was laying groundwork. She was making herself known, liked, and welcomed. When whatever she was planning came to pass, these people would remember her as that lovely young woman who'd been so interested in their wares and had made them feel important. They'd never even think of her as a hellkin. They'd never suspect her of anything nefarious.

A flash of movement in his peripheral vision made him turn.

For a moment, he was sure he'd spotted Erindil, but was the usually fussy elf in trousers and a tunic? Before he could get a good look, the figure with silvery hair had vanished behind one of the market stalls. He didn't have long to dwell on it, as he spied Fenni approaching the market from the direction of his cheese shop and heading straight for where Marina was currently examining bulbs of garlic.

Without thinking, Vaskel intercepted the cheesemonger, stepping directly into his path with what he hoped was a casual smile. "Fenni! Just the halfling I was hoping to see."

The cheesemonger stopped, tugging the points of his red plaid waistcoat to extend over his belly and meet his perfectly coordinated red pants. Trust Fenni to be impeccably dressed even for a simple trip to the market. "What a pleasant surprise, Vaskel. What can I do for you?"

"I was wondering about your winter cheeses," Vaskel said, positioning himself so Fenni's back was to Marina. "The tavern could use something special for the wedding feast."

Fenni's face lit up as he rubbed his chubby hands together. "Oh, you've come to the right person! I've just received the most extraordinary shipment. There's a soft cheese from the Skittering Islands that's been aged in volcanic caves—it gives it this wonderful mineral quality that pairs beautifully with winter fruits."

Vaskel nodded encouragingly, sneaking glances over Fenni's shoulder to track Marina's progress through the market. She'd moved on from the garlic vendor and was now examining leather goods with the tanner.

"And then," Fenni continued, warming to his subject, "there's a particularly fine hard cheese from the borderlands. They age it for a minimum of three years, and it develops these wonderful crystalline patches that crunch when you bite into them. The flavor is nutty and complex with just a hint of caramel at the finish."

"That sounds perfect," Vaskel said, though his attention was split between Fenni's enthusiastic description and Marina's movements. She was getting closer to the edge of the market now, near where it opened onto the main road.

Fenni launched into a detailed explanation of optimal serving temperatures and pairing suggestions, his hands fluttering as he spoke. Any other day, Vaskel would have been genuinely interested. After all, Fenni's cheese knowledge was encyclopedic. But right now, all he could focus on was keeping the halfling distracted long enough for Marina to move on.

"—and if you serve it with a drizzle of that honey from the Elmshire hives, it creates this incredible harmony of flavors that—"

"I'll take both," Vaskel interrupted, relief flooding through him as he saw Marina leaving the market and striding down the main road toward the castle. "Two wheels of each for the wedding."

Fenni beamed. "Excellent choice! Oh, Lira and Korl are going to have such a magnificent feast!"

"I'm sure they will," Vaskel agreed, already backing away. "Thanks, Fenni. I should get to the tavern before Sass comes looking for me."

Fenni's thick eyebrows popped high. "Goodness, we don't want that." He shooed him away with a grin. "Go, go!"

Vaskel let out a relieved sigh as Fenni headed into the market. Guilt gnawed gently at him for using Sass as an excuse, but the dwarf *could* be formidable when irritated. Now that he thought about it, he should hurry to work before he incurred a scolding for being so late.

As he turned to leave, his gaze snagged on something red. Turning back, he spotted a hellkin leaning against a market stall peddling root vegetables. But it wasn't Marina. This hellkin hadn't bothered to disguise himself to blend in. He wore a dark cloak to ward off the cold, but one side flapped open to reveal the steely glint of a blade at his waist.

Vaskel met the hellkin's eyes and narrowed his own. This was clearly one of Marina's young recruits, no doubt sent to spy on Vaskel and send him a message. Well, Vaskel could send a message of his own.

Cocking his head, he touched one hand to his forehead and mimed tipping an imaginary hat to the young hellkin, even smirking at him. This provoked exactly the scowl Vaskel had wanted.

Taking long strides away from the market and the hellkin, past the stone monument centering the village, and through the shops on both sides of the main road, Vaskel didn't glance over his shoulder once. Even though he pretended to be nonchalant about the appearance of hellkins in Wayside, he was deep in his own thoughts. How could he warn the villagers without causing a panic or revealing the truth of his connection to her?

He'd almost reached Pip's bakery, reminding himself that he didn't have time to stop this morning, when he stopped dead in his tracks.

There, near the stone bridge that crossed the stream, stood Marina. But she wasn't alone. She was deep in conversation with someone, one of her crimson hand's resting lightly on his arm.

Vaskel's stomach sank as Marina shifted and he spotted who was behind her. Thrain.

The dwarf stared at her, transfixed, his usually gruff expression replaced with the dopey smile of someone completely under a hellkin's spell.

Marina laughed at something Thrain said, the sound dancing between them in the frigid air, and she leaned closer to the dwarf, her crimson hand squeezing his arm. Vaskel felt a phantom pulse on his own arm, so sharp was the memory of Marina touching him in the same intoxicating, possessive way.

Thrain, who'd bravely ventured from his home in the Ice Lands to warn Sass of danger and who hadn't flinched in the face of battle, appeared completely enchanted by the beautiful hellkin.

There wasn't a shred of doubt in Vaskel's mind that Marina was using Thrain as part of her sinister plan, just as there was nothing Vaskel could do about it without revealing everything.

83

Eighteen

FRUSTRATION BURNED through Vaskel's veins as he watched Marina lead Thrain over the bridge and toward the castle. He could run after them, but what would he say? He knew Marina well enough to know that she would plead innocence, and he would look like a fool. Every instinct screamed at him to race after his friend, grab Thrain by the shoulders, and shake him until he saw Marina for what she really was. But it would be pointless.

He'd crewed with Marina long enough to know her patterns, her weaknesses, her talents. And the one thing Marina savored more than anything else was taking something someone else loved. If she discovered Thrain was important to him, that the gruff dwarf had become a friend he genuinely cared about, she'd sink her claws in deeper. She'd hurt him just to hurt Vaskel.

No, the best thing, really the only thing he could do to keep his friends safe was to break the hells-cursed soul bind. He needed to cut Marina's hold over him completely and permanently. Then and only then would his friends be safe.

His boots crunched over the foot-worn snow with unnecessary force as he resumed walking, barely noticing the door to the tinker shop creaking open as he passed. He glanced over as Korl emerged, ducking slightly to clear the low doorframe. The orc had only recently given up his position as guardsman to reopen the old shop, though Vaskel knew he still helped Val with patrols occasionally. Today, though, he wore no armor. Thick brown pants encased his massive legs, topped with what had to be the most peculiar sweater Vaskel had ever seen.

The cream-colored garment was warm-looking, but lumpy in odd places, with one arm that reached past Korl's wrist and another that barely made it halfway down his forearm. The neck was too loose, exposing plenty of green chest, and there appeared to be an extra hole near the shoulder that served no discernible purpose.

Vaskel stopped mid-stride, doing a double take that made Korl's dark eyes crinkle with what might have been amusement.

"Val made it," the orc explained before Vaskel could formulate a question about the sweater. "Before she decided she should stick to scarves."

Despite everything consuming his thoughts and darkening his mood, Vaskel grinned. "It looks warm."

Korl grunted, a sound that landed somewhere between agreement and resignation. "It is that." He raised the short arm, displaying how it only reached halfway down his forearm, leaving his wrist and hand exposed to the winter air. "In most places."

Vaskel was unable to contain his laughter as he shook his head. "I will never question why Val only knits scarves again."

"Heading to The Tusk & Tail?" Korl asked, falling into step beside him when Vaskel nodded. "Mind if I walk with you?"

"I'd be glad for the company," Vaskel said, and meant it. Korl's solid, quiet presence was exactly what he needed right now.

They walked in companionable silence for several moments, their heavy footsteps crackling rhythmically through the snow. The village was fully awake now, smoke rising from every chimney, the aroma of yeast tinging the air, and the sounds of daily life drifting from open doors and windows.

"Something on your mind?" Korl's deep voice broke through the hellkin's dark thoughts.

Vaskel started, surprised that the orc had noticed his distraction. But then, quiet folk always noticed things others missed. They observed instead of filling every silence with words.

"Thought it was grooms who were supposed to be anxious about weddings," Korl added.

Vaskel shook his head, grateful the orc hadn't discerned the truth. "I'm not nervous about your wedding, if that's what you're thinking. I'm thrilled to be part of it. Honored that you asked me to stand with you."

Another grunt from Korl, this one somehow conveying different emotions than the one before it. "You've been a good friend. To Lira and to me."

The simple words hit Vaskel harder than they should have. Korl wasn't one for speeches or declarations, which made his spare words carry more weight.

"If there's ever any way I can be a friend to you," Korl continued, his gaze fixed ahead as if eye contact might make the offer too heavy, "you only need ask."

They'd reached the tavern now, stopping beneath the wooden sign that swayed gently in the winter breeze and creaked lazily on old hinges.

Vaskel put a hand on Korl's shoulder. "Thank you. That means more than you know."

The villagers of Wayside—Korl, Pip, Sass, all of them—had started as Lira's friends, her chosen family after returning home, but somewhere along the way, without him noticing, they'd become his as well. Not because he'd charmed them or seduced them or manipulated them the way Marina would have. But simply because he'd been there, working alongside them, sharing their joys and troubles, and becoming part of the fabric of their daily lives.

"I'm fine," he added, wishing it were true. "But if I need a friend, I'll come to you. I promise." He forced a grin. "What about you? Any nerves about the big day?"

Korl's expression shifted, his brow smoothing and a shy smile teasing the corners of his mouth. "My only worry is that Erindil's ostrich will drink all the brandy again." He counted off on his fingers. "That Lira's flutterstoat will insist on riding on her shoulder down the aisle. And that my dads will cry so loudly no one will hear the ceremony." He tugged open the tavern door, warm air and the scent of baking spilling out. "Normal stuff."

Vaskel followed him inside, laughing and shaking his head at the orc's deadpan delivery. "Normal stuff, indeed."

Nineteen

THE TUSK & Tail buzzed with chatter as Sass worked the crowd, doling out afternoon scones while Vaskel pulled the occasional pint for those patrons who didn't prefer chai. It should have been comforting, this familiar hum of conversation, but Vaskel couldn't shake the knot of tension coiled in his stomach.

He'd been scanning the tavern all day, looking for one particular dwarf among the many faces. Usually, Thrain would hold court at one of the long tables, his voice booming over the general din as he munched on scones and regaled anyone within earshot with increasingly elaborate tales. But now, there was no sign of him.

"Remember that time in Port Frey?" Rog had claimed the stool directly across from Vaskel, crumbly bits of scone littering his blue beard. "When you convinced that merchant you were a traveling duke?"

"Mmm," Vaskel responded, mindlessly polishing a pewter mug while his eyes swept the room again.

"You had him so convinced, he gave us free room and board for a week." Rog chuckled. "Course, we had to leave town pretty quick when the real duke showed up."

"Right." Vaskel forced a smile, but his attention was elsewhere. Where was Thrain? More importantly, where was Marina? The two had been together this morning, and they'd been heading down the road that led to Grayhelm Castle. If the dwarf didn't reappear soon, Vaskel would need to mount a search.

"You're not listening to a word I'm saying, are you?" Rog's voice held amusement rather than offense.

"Sorry," Vaskel stopped polishing the sparkling mug. "Long day."

Rog studied him with sharp eyes that missed nothing, despite his jovial demeanor. "Anything you want to talk about?"

Before Vaskel could plan a response that wasn't a complete lie, the door opened with a burst of cold air. His head snapped up, but it was only Tinpin, shaking snow from his burgundy coat.

"Looking for someone?" Rog asked, his blue brows lifting.

"Just keeping an eye on the patrons." Vaskel moved down the bar to get a clean dishcloth, not bothering to look when the door opened and closed again.

Then he breathed in the scent of bergamot and herbs, turning to see Iris approaching the bar, her dark curls pinned up in a loose bun that was already beginning to escape its coil, wisps framing her face. She wore a deep green dress instead of her usual patchwork skirts, and something in his chest tightened at the sight of her.

"A moment?" she said as she walked past.

He nodded, moving to the far end of the bar where there were fewer customers.

When they were as alone as they could be in the bustling tavern, she hopped onto a stool and leaned over the bar. "You snuck out before I woke up."

"And you didn't wake me when I drifted off in your armchair," he replied.

She smiled at this. "You were clearly exhausted. Besides, it was a good excuse for me to grab a few winks."

He glanced at the sun shining through the windows. "Did you just wake up?"

She shook her head with a chuckle. "As if the villagers would let me. But when I haven't been doling out throat tonics and healing powders, I've been scouring more books."

"Any solutions?"

She bit her bottom lip as she met his gaze. "No, but I came to the realization that we need help."

He opened his mouth to argue, but she held up a hand. "We don't have to tell all your friends, but I can't ignore the fact that we have an elf in our midst. He helped when Sass had a magical issue. We would be foolish not to ask for his insight."

She was right. It would be foolish to ignore Erindil's abilities. Even if he couldn't wield magic like a trained mage, elves possessed natural powers and highly tuned perception.

"Agreed." He nodded, but the movement and his voice were wooden. Iris cocked her head at him, a question that didn't need a voice.

"Marina was in the market this morning," he said, his voice barely above a whisper. "She'd shed her usual attire and was trying to blend in as a villager."

"She's no longer hiding?"

Vaskel shrugged. "She's unpredictable, but it's all part of her plan. Just like charming Thrain."

Iris's eyes widened slightly. "Sass's friend? That Thrain?"

"Who else?" he said, frustration making his words sharp. "She's using him for something. To get to me, most likely."

The thought that Marina could have been watching him and observing who his friends were made anger roil in his chest.

"We won't let anyone get hurt," Iris said, and her hand found his on the bar, cool fingers wrapping around his clenched fist. The touch sent a jolt through him that had nothing to do with the soul bind.

Then the door opened again. This time, it was Thrain.

Relief flooded through Vaskel so powerfully his knees almost buckled. Then the relief died in his throat.

Marina stepped through the door right behind Thrain, shaking snowflakes from her dark hair. She still wore her village disguise, but the modest brown dress couldn't hide what she was, not from someone who knew her true nature.

Thrain said something that made her laugh again, the sound cutting through the tavern noise like a blade through silk. Several heads turned, both men's and women's faces going slack with appreciation, and only a very few sharpening with the instinctive wariness prey feels when a hunter enters their territory.

Marina's gaze swept the room, cataloguing exits, threats, and opportunities like she always did. Like Vaskel himself did instinctively after decades of adventuring. It took her less than three seconds to locate him at the bar.

Their eyes locked before her gaze dropped to where Iris's hand still rested on his. Marina's lips curved into a smile like a predator discovering exactly the weakness she'd been looking for. The temperature in the tavern seemed to drop ten degrees despite the crackling fire.

Vaskel jerked his hand back and turned away, but it was too late. Marina had seen, and now she's discovered an even more powerful weapon to use against him.

Twenty

THRAIN MOVED THROUGH THE TAVERN, Marina draped on his arm. The dwarf's chest puffed with pride as he introduced her to table after table of villagers.

"This is Marina," Thrain announced. "Just arrived in Wayside yesterday, looking for a place to winter."

Marina ducked her head with perfectly feigned shyness, her crimson skin glowing in the firelight. "Everyone's been so welcoming. I can see why Thrain speaks so highly of this village."

Vaskel curled his hands into fists. This was Marina at her most dangerous. She wielded charm as deftly as she did blades, and Vaskel knew how skilled she was with both.

"You should probably leave," Vaskel murmured to Iris.

She lifted her chin, green eyes flashing. "I'm not afraid of her. And I'm certainly not going to be run out of the tavern in *my* village."

Before he could argue, Sass appeared at his side behind the bar, one hand planted firmly on her hip, her eyes narrowed to slits as she watched Marina wind her way through the room.

"I don't like her," the dwarf said. "Don't trust her as far as I could throw her, and considering she's twice my size, that's not bloody far."

A grin tugged at his lips. Trust Sass to see through Marina's artifice.

"Something about her makes my skin crawl," Sass continued. "Thrain's a goblin-spawned fool if he can't see she's playing him like a fiddle. Sweet simmering cauldrons, the way she's got him prancing about like a prize pig at market."

For the first time since he'd met the dwarf, he was grateful she was immune to hellkin charm. Vaskel remembered his own failed attempts to win her over when he'd first arrived, despite his best efforts to charm her. She'd looked at him with the same suspicious squint she was now directing at Marina.

"Where in Grognick's beard have you been?" Lira emerged from the kitchen carrying a tray laden with steaming meat pies, her face flushed from the heat of the ovens. "These have been ready for ages!"

"Sorry," Sass muttered, still glaring at Marina. "Got distracted."

Lira followed their collective gaze across the room, her eyes widening as she took in the scene. "Who is that?"

Iris glanced at Vaskel, a question in her eyes. Should they tell her? Should they warn everyone about what Marina really was, what she was capable of? Then Vaskel thought of Lira's upcoming wedding. He didn't want to be the one to steal her joy with his problems.

"Just a newcomer Thrain brought in," Iris said smoothly. "Apparently she's looking for somewhere to spend the winter."

"Thrain has always been a soft-hearted fool," Sass grumbled, taking the tray from Lira with more force than necessary.

"Which is why he came all the way from the Ice Lands looking for you, right?" Lira teased.

Sass harrumphed, her cheeks darkening slightly. "That's different. We've been friends since we were no taller than a battle axe." She flicked a hand in Marina's direction. "She's a stranger."

Lira shook her head at Sass's grumbling and headed back to the kitchen. Sass stomped off with the meat pies, deliberately taking the long way around the room to avoid passing near Marina and Thrain.

Iris gave Vaskel a reassuring smile before she left through the crowd, carefully avoiding Marina's line of sight. Vaskel watched her go, then turned his attention back to Marina, who was playfully tugging Rog's blue beard while the gnome blushed furiously. His wife would have Marina's head if she saw this, but Rosie must still be tucked away in their wooden wagon.

The marks on Vaskel's skin pulsed with heat as Marina flicked her gaze away from Rog to catch his eyes. She was showing him exactly how easily she could get to him through those he cared about.

He snatched his gaze away, suppressing a growl. He knew what he needed to do.

"You mind covering for me for a bit?" Vaskel asked Sass when she returned to the bar, her gaze still tracking Marina and Thrain like a hawk watching a snake slither closer to its nest.

She nodded without glancing at him. "You go. I'll keep an eye on those two."

The disgust in her voice when she said 'those two' would have made him smile under different circumstances. Now, he just needed to slip out before Marina noticed his absence.

Keeping to the walls, he edged toward the tavern door, sneaking out when Marina was pretending to laugh at one of Thrain's bad dwarf jokes. He took a beat to scan the empty road and woods. Vaskel knew Marina well enough to know that she could have her new crew posted as lookouts. Every shadow could hide a potential ambush.

He hadn't even reached the corner of the tavern when goose flesh tickled the back of his neck. He felt the distinctive prickle of being watched, of footsteps matching his own pace so they wouldn't be heard.

Marina. She'd noticed him leave. She was toying with him, letting him know she could follow him anywhere, that there was nowhere in Wayside he could hide from her. Fury and fear warred in his chest as he whirled around, ready to confront her, to tell her to leave his friends alone, to—

"Hells, Vask!" Lira jumped back as he almost slammed into her. "I thought I was jumpy. You want to tell me what's going on?"

Lira. Of course it was Lira. The half-elf had always been able to move like a shadow, and she'd always seemed to know when her friends were hiding something.

He exhaled slowly, his heart still hammering against his ribs. He'd come to Wayside looking for her because he'd known, bone-deep, that he could trust her with his life. They'd saved each other more times than he could count, and she'd never judged him for being a hellkin. She'd never treated him as anything other than her friend.

And now he needed to trust her again.

He took her hand in his. "I need to tell you something."

Twenty-One

LIRA GAPED AT HIM, her mouth opening and closing. Of all the reactions Vaskel had expected once he'd told her the entire story, stunned silence hadn't been one of them. After all, they'd encountered plenty of shocking situations when they ran together, and a soul bind hardly felt more startling than a horde of wraiths.

Finally, Lira grabbed his wrist and yanked his sleeve up to reveal the marks.

"I always knew you wanted to get me out of my clothes," he tried to tease, but his voice cracked.

She rolled her eyes at him, and his attempt at levity died on his lips as they both stared at the marks that were black as char and curling up his arm like infernal script. They pulsed faintly with each heartbeat, as if they were alive.

"Why didn't you ever tell me about this?" Hurt threaded through her soft words. "About a soul bind?"

The guilt that had been gnawing at him for days intensified. She deserved better from him. Every member of their crew who'd trusted him, fought beside him, and risked their lives for him deserved better.

"By the time we formed our crew, I'd forgotten all about it. I convinced myself it was a silly promise made late one night after too much ale. I convinced myself it wasn't real, or maybe I just didn't want to think it was." He paused, trying to find the right words. "I changed so much from those early days. When I was young and impulsive and believed what others told me a hellkin should be. By the time I met you all, that person felt like a stranger and that past didn't feel like mine anymore."

Lira nodded slowly, and he saw the understanding in her eyes. Of course, she understood. She'd left Wayside as one person and returned as another. They all carried past versions of themselves.

"But you could have told me about these marks sooner."

"I'm not proud of parts of my past, but I'm proud of our quests, and I'm especially proud of who I've become in Wayside. I don't want anyone who knows me as Vaskel the friendly barkeep to see me differently. That's why I didn't tell you right away, and that's why I want to keep this from the rest of the village."

"They won't see you differently," Lira said.

Vaskel grunted. "They might if they knew everything, and I wouldn't blame them."

Lira looked like she was going to argue more, but she pulled his sleeve down with deliberate care, then gave a curt nod that was pure determination. "Okay then. How do we break this bind?" Her tone shifted, and he remembered that this was the voice of the fearless rogue who'd once picked the lock on a lich's tomb while the undead sorcerer slept ten feet away. "Or break the hellkin who put it on you."

Blood and ashes, he loved her fierce loyalty and the way she immediately shifted into protective mode. But Marina wasn't some lock to be picked or corrupt guard they could outsmart.

"Marina isn't easy to defeat." He shook his head. "She's had centuries to hone her skills, and she has a crew of young hellkins eager to prove themselves."

Lira bristled, and suddenly she looked less like a kindhearted tavernkeep who baked delicious scones and more like the dangerous rogue who'd fought by his side. "We still have most of our crew, plus Iris and—"

"No." He held up a hand, cutting her off. "I won't put the people I care about at risk. Not for my past mistakes."

"Vask." Her husky voice snapped him back to the present moment, and he saw that her hand was resting on his arm. "We're in this together. Just like always."

Like most hellkins, he kept his emotions under tight control, but he couldn't stop his throat from thickening as he smiled at her, nodding when he couldn't manage words.

"Even after what you know about my past?" He finally rasped. "Even after knowing I wasn't always so honorable?"

She squeezed his arm. "The mark of a great adventurer isn't a flawless quest. It's owning the wrong turns and still finding your way to the treasure."

He laughed at this. "Is that dwarf wisdom, by chance?"

Lira shook her head. "It sounds like it, doesn't it?" She took his sleeve and tugged. "Now come on, Vask."

"Where are we going?"

"We both know that Erindil has more power than anyone in Wayside and has been around longer than any of us. If anyone knows about soul binds, it will be him. Besides, if my uncle expects to have his ostrich in my wedding, he owes me." She took a steadying breath and met Vaskel's widening eyes. "Yes, I know about Glen and his outfit, and no, I'm not thrilled about it."

Vaskel walked briskly alongside her as Lira muttered about elves, deciding not to argue with his friend.

Twenty-Two

VASKEL HEARD the elf encampment before the colorful tents behind the tavern came into view. Lute music mixed with the warble of an ostrich and the gentle bubbling of voices overpowering the gurgle of the icy stream. The sun dipped below the trees, casting a pink glow over the snow-encrusted branches and dappling light onto the peaked tents arranged around a central fire.

Glen's head swung toward them as they trudged closer, his warble edging toward a screech. A tent flap adorned with gold tassels and elaborate embroidery fluttered open, and Erindil emerged in robes of thick white fur that made his silver blonde hair look even more ethereal.

"My dear niece! And the charming Vaskel!" His sharp features softened at the sight of them. "What a delightful surprise!"

He gestured grandly toward his tent. "You must join me inside. We can't have a proper conversation standing about in the cold."

Even though the camp wasn't as cold as the rest of the village thanks to an elvish enchantment, Vaskel followed the regal elf and Lira into the tent. The space was larger than it should have been, no doubt due to more elvish enchantment, and its opulence put any home in Wayside to shame. Lush carpets in deep jewel tones overlapped on the floor, with gilded furniture perched on top. Peacock feathers burst from vases like blooms, and Vaskel wouldn't have been surprised to see attendants fanning them.

Erindil settled into a high-backed chair, its gold leaf catching the light from the crystal chandelier suspended from the center of the tent. He gestured to a velvet tufted settee across from him, and Vaskel and Lira both sank into the cushioning, their knees almost bumping their ears.

Vaskel tried to adjust himself so he didn't tip over onto the carpets, but ended up settling on bracing himself with one arm with his tail curled around the furniture leg to catch him.

A few moments of silence passed before Erindil fastened his gaze on Vaskel and cleared his throat. "Dark magic again, is it?"

Vaskel shouldn't have been startled. After all, elves were known for their highly attuned intuition. He also suspected that after observing people for thousands of years, you'd become an expert at reading them. Still, it was unsettling to think that the elf sensed a darkness on him.

"No," Lira answered for him. "It's a soul bind."

"Ah." Erindil nodded deliberately, the twitching of his fingers the only sign of piqued interest. "May I see?"

There was no point in hesitating. Vaskel pushed up his sleeve, revealing the marks that wound up his arm like malevolent vines.

Erindil leaned forward, studying the marks and humming, occasionally tilting his head to view them from different angles. His fingers hovered above the marks but never quite touched, as if he didn't want to touch the enchantment.

"Fascinating," he murmured. "The binding work is quite sophisticated. Infernal power at its most intricate." Then he sat back, his fingers steepled under his chin. "I've seen this before."

Lira sagged with relief beside Vaskel, her shoulder bumping his. "You have?"

"Oh yes. Not often, mind you. Soul binds are old magic, the kind most modern hellkins have forgotten. But in my years..." He waved a hand vaguely, unwilling as always to specify exactly how many years those were. "Let's say I've encountered my share of ancient curses."

"Can you break it?" Vaskel asked, hope and desperation warring in his voice.

Erindil leaned back, curling his willowy fingers over the gold armrests of his chair. "It will not be easy to sever the bind, but..." He paused dramatically, because of course he did, "I might be able to do it."

Vaskel's heart lurched. "Might?"

Erindil drummed his fingers rhythmically. "I've never done it before, of course. Should I remind you I'm no mage, and my powers don't extend to infernal magic?" His stern expression relaxed into a hint of a smile. "Not that elvish enchantments are anything to sneeze at, and I'm more than willing to try. I will need use of the dear apothecary's workshop."

"Anything you need," Lira said immediately. "I know Iris would say the same. She's been working on this for days."

"Excellent." Erindil's attention returned to Vaskel, and something in his gaze sharpened. "But first, dear boy, I must know how you came to be bound. The nature of the binding, the circumstances, the one who holds the other end—these details matter immensely."

Vaskel sighed. He'd told this story to Iris and to Lira, but if confession was the price of freedom, he'd tell it a hundred times more. He opened his mouth to begin when an ostrich shriek split the air.

Vaskel and Lira wrestled with the settee and each other as they struggled to get to their feet. The last time they'd heard Glen screech like that, a dragon had been circling overhead.

 Twenty-Three

"SWEET, SIMMERING CAULDRONS!"

Vaskel was first out of the tent, grateful he'd resumed carrying a blade. His fingers danced above the dagger's hilt, but he was hesitant to brandish it before he scanned the camp for danger. His hand dropped when he realized that the only danger was Glen with his wings spread and his beady eyes locked onto something. That something was Rosie.

The gnome woman stood frozen mid-step, clutching a pair of glass jugs to her chest, her expression caught between confusion and irritation. A thick, blonde braid coiled around her head like a crown, and she wore a cheerful yellow apron.

It took only a moment to determine that the object of Glen's hysteria wasn't an intruder, but Rosie's brandy.

"Bloody, brandy-stealing bird," Rosie said, glaring at Glen with as much intensity as he was eyeing her brandy.

Erindil sighed as he stomped up to Glen, looking less like regal, centuries-old Elven royalty and more like a weary parent. "Remember what happened last time you got into Rosie's brandy?"

Glen's shriek morphed into what could only be described as a sulky warble. He tucked his wings back against his body but continued to eye the jug with unabashed longing.

Rosie shifted one of the glass containers onto her hip and shook a chubby finger at the ostrich. "Don't even think about it, you oversized chicken. This batch isn't for you." She turned to Lira, her round face breaking into a warm smile. "I was heading to the back door of the tavern to give these to you, but I might as well give them to you here."

Rosie and Rog's wagon was permanently parked between the elf encampment and the stone bridge, which meant that the quickest way to the back entrance of The Tusk & Tail was through the cluster of elf tents.

Lira blinked, clearly still coming down from the momentary panic of expecting danger. "For me? I don't think I can drink that much myself."

"Not for now, you goose!" Rosie said between giggles. "For your wedding! I've made a special apple brandy filled with winter spices and a hint of plum. I've been working on the recipe for weeks."

Relief washed across Lira's face for a beat before her brow pinched with concern. "That's so sweet, but you didn't have to make a special brandy just for us."

Rosie waved this off with the flap of one hand. "It's the

wedding of the year! The decade! Two of Wayside's own getting married is the biggest thing to happen to this village since, well..." She paused and winked. "Since Rog and I arrived."

Vaskel noticed Lira's cheeks pale as she nibbled her lower lip. He stepped forward and reached for the large glass jugs. "Why don't I take those? I can store them behind the bar until the wedding."

"Good man, hellkin, oh, you know," Rosie said, grinning at him and traversing the brandy into his arms. "I'd better get back to the wagon."

She ambled away, as Lira mumbled her own excuses and rushed toward the tavern's back door.

Erindil followed his niece's quick departure with one cocked, patrician eyebrow. "Should I...?"

"I'll check on her," Vaskel told him, already moving to the tavern. "I need to tuck these away, anyway."

"Yes, yes." Erindil slid his battle ostrich a quelling look. "Far away from prying ostrich eyes, if you please." As he turned and led Glen back toward his tent, he held Vaskel's gaze for a beat. "But find me later. I still want to know more about your soul bind."

Vaskel muttered his agreement and a vague promise about coming back later, but he pushed both from his mind as soon as he entered the tavern. He ignored the growing crowd and even the fact that Val was behind the bar as Sass bustled around the long tables. Keeping his head low, he tucked the jugs of brandy behind the bar and headed for where he was sure he'd find Lira.

But when he pushed through the swinging kitchen doors, he stopped short. Instead of Lira busily baking, she was standing frozen at the stove while Crumpet stirred a burbling pot, while Bramble the raccoon was using his deft little paws to fold pastry into half-moon shaped pies.

"Hells and cinders," he muttered with a shake of his head.

Before he could address Lira and her obvious reaction to the wedding brandy, Sass burst in behind him.

"What in Grognick's beard is going on in here?" She flipped her dark braid off her shoulder, leveling a finger at Vaskel. "You should be behind the bar before Val over-serves everyone in the place."

He hesitated, but Lira seemed to snap herself out of whatever spiral the wedding brandy had sent her into, taking the spoon from Crumpet so the flutterstoat could sag against her.

"First you leave," Sass flapped her hand at Vaskel, clearly not done with him. "Then Lira hares off after you. Then a pair of hellkins not nearly as charming as you, tried to get out of paying with some poorly veiled threats."

"Hellkins?" Vaskel's mouth went dry. Festering dragon dung! He hoped Marina would keep her crew away from Wayside. That had obviously been wishful thinking on his part.

Sass huffed out a breath. "Nothing I couldn't handle. I told them to pay up, or I'd send some trolls after them."

"That's our Sass," Lira said with a grin. "Always quick on her feet."

The dwarf shook a severe finger at her. "Don't try to get back on my good side. You left me with a kitchen staff of wee beasties. If you'd been gone much longer, I would have had to borrow a badger from the forest to help clear tables."

Vaskel watched Lira's brows lift and thought that Sass had better be careful what outlandish things she said or she might indeed find a badger working in the tavern one morning.

"It won't happen again," Lira assured her, which prompted a few more grumbles from the dwarf.

"I'll get back to the bar," Vaskel said, with a last look at Lira. He'd have to wait until later to thank her for keeping his secret and for taking him to see her uncle.

"You'll be glad to know that the dodgy hellkin is gone," Sass said with a satisfied nod, which faded quickly. "But so is Thrain."

Vaskel rushed out to the great room, his gaze scanning the tables filled with patrons. No Marina and no Thrain.

He huffed out a breath. "Festering goblin spawn."

Twenty-Four

VASKEL SLUMPED FARTHER DOWN in the overstuffed armchair and dragged the pewter tankard to his lips, sipping the ale that was no longer cold. "He'll be back soon."

Val sank into the chair across from his, the impact making the yarn basket on the floor jump and her own ale slosh over the lip of the tankard. "You can't stay here all night waiting for Thrain."

"He has to come back at some point," Vaskel mumbled, more into his drink than to Val.

Val gave him a broad grin and raised her ale in salute. "To Thrain returning."

Vaskel didn't bother to lift his drink before taking another swig. The tavern had emptied out long enough ago that Sass had swept the floors twice. Even the fire was a pile of murmuring embers glowing orange in the stone hearth.

Korl and Lira emerged hand-in-hand from the kitchen, both doing a double-take to see so many people left around the fire after closing.

Sass sauntered up with the bristle broom in one hand. "You truly intend to stay here until he returns?"

"Until who returns?" Lira asked.

"Thrain." Vaskel flicked his gaze to the back staircase that led to both Sass's bedroom and Thrain's. "He sleeps here. That means he has to come back."

"We can wait with you," Lira said, although she didn't sound excited by the prospect.

"The last thing we need is a sleep-deprived bride." Sass propped her broom against the nearest table and perched on the arm of Val's chair. "You should go home."

"You're just saying that because I've been in a mood the past few days," Lira said.

"Mood?" Val attempted a look of disbelief while Vaskel shook his head with an unrealistic amount of enthusiasm.

Korl scratched the side of his head. "Have you?"

A laugh burst from Lira. "You are all horrid actors. The worst."

"Don't look at me." Sass held up both palms. "I'm not pretending you haven't been in a wedding funk."

"I know it's silly to let wedding planning steal my joy about actually getting married." She tipped her face to Korl's. "You know that my mood has nothing to do with wanting to marry you, because I really, really do."

He cupped her face in one large, green hand. "And you know that none of the frills matter to me at all. We could get married right now in front of this fireplace, and I'd be just as happy."

Her eyes shone with tears. "Me too."

"Too bad we don't have a cleric nearby or we could save ourselves a lot of headaches," Sass mumbled, and Val gave her a gentle shove.

"I promise not to worry about the things that don't matter anymore." Lira popped up on her tiptoes and gave Korl a soft kiss. "If Erindil is dying to have Glen be a ring bearer, who cares?"

Sass opened her mouth, but Val yanked her into her lap on the chair to silence her.

Korl's cheeks darkened, and he cleared his throat. "Maybe we should head home."

Vaskel flapped a hand at them. "Go. You don't need to wait for Thrain with me."

"If you're sure..." Lira said with a breathless giggle as Korl pulled her toward the door.

Val sighed as they ran into the night, and even Sass was grinning and sliding looks to her girlfriend.

"You two don't need to stay either," Vaskel said, his gaze falling to Val's knitting. "I'm sure you have better things to do than help me fix a mess I made long ago."

Val held up her knitting. "Even the most tangled skein of yarn can be fixed if you're patient enough to work on the knots."

Vaskel suspected the woman was talking about more than knitting scarves.

"I don't see how Thrain has anything to do with your past." Sass made a sound in the back of her throat. "Thrain's his own dwarf, and he's never been one to make the best decisions when it comes to ladies, but I doubt you could stop him."

Vaskel glowered at Sass. "Marina is no lady."

"I know why I don't like her," Sass said. "Why don't you?"

Val squinted at Vaskel, as if trying to focus on his face. Then she curled an arm around Sass. "Good question, love."

The dwarf smiled at Val, leaning into her and brushing a strand of blonde hair from the woman's forehead. "Thanks, babe."

Vaskel watched the couple gaze at each other for a moment. If he hadn't had so much to drink, he would have looked away, but he couldn't help grinning at the unlikely pair. If a dwarf and a woman with Goliath blood could be happy, maybe he and—

Sass's gaze snapped back to Vaskel, interrupting his meandering thoughts. "Why don't you like the mysterious stranger? Don't hellkins get along with each other?"

Vaskel grunted. "Depends on the hellkins, but Marina is no stranger."

Sass and Val exchanged a look, and Sass leaned toward Vaskel. "Who is she?"

Vaskel realized too late that he'd said too much. He pressed his lips into a tight line as he stared into the dying embers, thinking of Thrain out there somewhere with Marina. He stroked one hand down his short beard. Maybe if he'd said something earlier, the dwarf would be tucked safely in his bed upstairs.

He huffed out a breath. "Long before I knew Lira or Cali or any of the crew you know, I ran with Marina."

Sass sat back, taking Val's ale and downing a gulp. "I take it you weren't the kind of crew who became family."

Vaskel shook his head, and his long hair swung around his face. "We weren't, and it wasn't a crew that took noble quests."

"We all have a past, Vask," Val said, her voice low.

He gave a gruff nod. "I thought I'd left my past far behind me. It had been so long—decades—since I'd heard from Marina. I thought, no, I hoped, that she'd forgotten me."

"So, she's here because of you?" Sass asked, handing Val back her ale.

Vaskel set his nearly empty tankard on the floor and held out his arm with a mournful shake of his head. "No, she's here because of this." He shoved up his sleeve to reveal the black marks coiling up his arm. "She's here because I was young and foolish and agreed to a soul bind in exchange for powers."

Sass almost fell off the arm of the chair as she tipped forward, but Val caught her around the waist.

"What is that?" The dwarf's voice held no edge.

Vaskel flopped back in the chair. "A soul bind, and Marina is here to collect."

"Collect how?" Val asked in a hush.

"I have to leave with her, join her new crew, do her bidding. I have three days, well, now only two, to say my farewells."

Sass snatched her gaze from the marks. "Then why is she interested in Thrain?"

"She isn't. She's only interested in the leverage he might have over me."

"She knows you don't want to leave Wayside," Val said, her expression pained as she looked at Vaskel. "She knows you're happy here, so she has to let you know she can get to your friends if you don't leave."

Vaskel's throat was too tight for him to reply, but he managed a brusque nod.

He chanced a glance at Sass. As expected, her expression was thunderous. Not that he blamed her for being mad at him. It was his fault Thrain was out there with Marina.

Sass stood and squared her shoulders. "If that hellkin thinks she can come in here and threaten one of us, she's sorely mistaken."

He blinked at her. "You're not angry at me?"

"For being young and making a dumb mistake?" Sass snorted.

"Join the club," Val said, bobbing her head in agreement.

"You aren't upset that I didn't tell you sooner?"

Sass unleashed a long sigh. "I know what it's like to have a past you want to hide, which is why I would never judge you for also having one."

"Even if my past is darker?"

"Aye, even so." Sass gave him a fierce grin. "You're not your past, Vaskel. None of us are. Now tell us everything about this curse and the moldy ogre's sack of a hellkin who gave it to you."

Twenty-Five

VASKEL'S NECK protested violently as he shifted, and he awoke suddenly when he realized he was still in the overstuffed armchair.

The fire that had bristled with flames when he'd been talking with Sass and Val was now a cold pile of dusky ash, and the chair where they'd been sitting was empty. The last thing he remembered was telling the dwarf and the guardswoman everything he knew about the soul bind, Marina, and everyone else in Wayside who knew.

He glanced at the back staircase, his heart pounding. How had he allowed himself to fall asleep before Thrain returned? Had Thrain returned?

The hellkin did his best to hurry across the great room and up the stairs, even though his legs were too stiff for him to take them two at a time. He paused at Sass's door, peeking inside to assure himself that she was still safe.

Sure enough, Val was curled around the smaller form of Sass, although both of them were on top of the floral coverlet and wearing the same clothes they'd had on the night before. They must have dragged themselves upstairs and been too tired to do anything but collapse.

Pulling the door shut as quietly as he could, Vaskel stepped quickly to Thrain's room, pausing for a moment and holding his breath before opening the door. His breath escaped him in a desperate rush when he spied the dwarf sprawled on top of his bed, his arms splayed wide and his whiskers fluttering as he snored loud enough to wake the undead. After hours of worry, he couldn't stop the half laugh, half sob that burst from his lips.

"Wh-what?" Thrain jerked awake, spluttering on a snore and jerking to sitting. He blinked hard as he focused on Vaskel, finally shaking his head. "Vask?"

Suddenly, Vaskel realized he didn't have a reason for being in Thrain's room. Not one he could tell the dwarf. Not yet. Not before he was sure how deep his friend was under Marina's spell.

"I was worried about you." This was true. "You were out so late."

Thrain dragged a hand through his dark, wiry beard before cocking his head. "Didn't know I had a curfew."

Vaskel's face warmed. Fretting about his friends comings and goings wasn't something he'd ever done, which made it even more awkward that he'd invaded the dwarf's bedroom so early. "Sorry, I—"

Vaskel barked a laugh. "I'm pulling your leg, laddie. If you must know, I was with Marina, the newcomer I introduced around the tavern last night."

Vaskel bit the inside of his mouth to keep from saying something about Marina he'd regret. "Where did you go when you left the tavern? Is she staying nearby?"

Vaskel would love to know if Marina and her new hellkin crew were camping in the woods or if they'd taken over a cottage after dispensing with the occupants. He knew for certain they weren't at the Wayside Inn, which was the only place in town with rooms to let.

"You could say that." Thrain swung his feet over the side of the bed, and they almost touched the floor. "She's a guest at Greyhelm Castle."

This surprised Vaskel. "The castle?" Had Marina befriended the ailing laird in the past two decades? "She's not related to the laird."

Thrain chuckled. "Aye, there aren't any hellkin lairds. No, she's the guest of the castle since she's a renowned healer. She's come to help the dying laird."

The old ruler of Greyhelm Castle had been on death's door for so long that Vaskel doubted there was anything a true healer, much less a fake one like Marina, could do for him. A scowl tugged at his mouth as he thought of Marina's cunning charm and the false hope she was giving a dying man.

The dwarf smacked his forehead with one meaty hand. "But why am I telling you this? You know her."

Vaskel froze. Every muscle in his body went rigid as ice stilled his veins. What had Marina told him? About their past, their crew, the things they'd done together? They'd done questionable things when they were young and running with a hellkin crew—theft, deception, acts that skirted the edge of darkness. Things Vaskel had spent years trying to forget, to atone for, to leave behind.

He waited for Thrain's shock, for disgust to replace the enthusiasm, for the dwarf to back away from him with the wariness reserved for someone who'd learned an ugly truth.

Instead, Thrain continued cheerfully, "She says she knew you from way back, when you were younglings."

Relief flooded through Vaskel so suddenly his knees went watery. Marina hadn't revealed their actual connection, although he knew all too well that it was for her own benefit that she hid the truth, not his.

Vaskel supposed it was partially true. He'd been close to a youngling when they'd first crewed together, barely past his coming of age and drunk on freedom. He'd been young enough to make terrible decisions that would haunt him decades later.

He brushed the bitterness from his voice. "It's been a long time since I'd seen her. We've both changed a great deal."

Thrain's expression shifted, becoming more serious, and he slid off the bed. "I need to know if you have any claims on her, Vask."

Claims on Marina? It was so completely backward that he almost choked. She was the one who had bound his very soul to hers, marked him like property, and held the tether that could drag him back to a life he'd abandoned.

"I assure you I have none." The fact that the same couldn't be said about her made his marks flare hot.

Thrain thumped him hard on one arm. "Glad to hear it." He winked. "I'd have hated to fight you for her."

Before Vaskel could think of a response or work out a way to warn Thrain in a way that the lovesick dwarf wouldn't reject as outright lies, his friend had pushed past him and was lumbering down the stairs.

Vaskel blew out a hot breath. At least he'd learned something. Marina had ensconced herself in the castle. Then his tail twitched, an unmistakable warning as he remembered what else was at the castle and what could befall all of them if Marina discovered the secret in the dungeons.

Twenty-Six

VASKEL TRUDGED DOWN THE STAIRS, still working through arguments to use on Thrain. The great room was empty, and he groaned at the thought that Thrain had already left to meet up with Marina. If only he didn't understand all too well the intoxicating magnetism the female hellkin possessed.

Before he could pop his head into the kitchen or prepare the bar for the day ahead, the back door of the tavern swung open, and a figure bedecked in furs swept inside, bringing cold air and a torrent of snow flurries with him.

Erindil flung back his fur hood. "I've had an idea!" Then his voice dropped to a conspiratorial whisper that was still carried across the great room. "About your personal issue."

Vaskel flinched. The way Erindil said it made it sound like he had a rash in his nether regions, and he was profoundly grateful that the tavern was empty.

"A cure?" Vaskel asked as the elf glided toward him, the train of his white fur coat trailing behind him.

"Cure would be too strong a word, since I'm not certain it will work. But I did recall a similar soul bind from a few hundred—or was it a thousand?—years ago. It was a terrible business, but in this case a hellkin had put the soul bind on a troll. Don't ask me why anyone would want to be bound to a troll..."

Erindil took him by the elbow and steered him from the tavern and down the snow-crusted road. They were moving so fast that Vaskel's longer legs were actually working to keep up with the elf's surprising speed.

The waterwheel splashed into the stream, and the blacksmith's forge belched out black smoke as they passed, but Vaskel was grateful that Vorto and Klaff were not outside to see him rushing by with Lira's uncle.

"The key," Erindil continued, although now his whisper was actually a whisper, "is in the strategy. Not breaking the bind so much as unwinding it, like untangling a particularly stubborn knot. But we'll need our apothecary friend's workshop. She has ingredients I couldn't possibly—"

"Morning!" Fenni leaned out of his cheese shop door, the halfling's eyebrows raised in question at their hurried pace.

Vaskel flashed what he hoped was his most convincing smile. "Good morning!" Then he added. "Wedding business."

Fenni's face lit up with understanding, and he waved them on. "Carry on!"

Erindil didn't even slow as he burst through the apothecary's door, the bell jangling violently. A woman at the counter let out a startled yelp, nearly dropping the bottle she'd been holding. A bottle Vaskel recognized to be the oil Iris prescribed for stomach troubles.

"My deepest, most profound apologies, my fine lady!" Erindil swept into an elaborate bow without releasing Vaskel's arm. "A thousand pardons for startling you. Please, don't let us interrupt."

The poor woman clutched the bottle and her coin purse, looking between them with wide eyes, as Erindil smiled at her with manic brightness. Vaskel took pity on her, pulling free from Erindil's grip to hold open the door.

The woman shoved some copper bits at Iris and fled, with her face flushed as crimson as Vaskel's.

"Lock the door," Erindil commanded, already turning to Iris, who stood behind her counter with an expression of bewildered irritation. "We have work to do."

Iris blinked several times, looking between the elf and the hellkin. "What—"

"He knows," Vaskel said simply, turning the lock with a definitive click. "About the soul bind."

"Ah." Understanding dawned on Iris's face. "And I assume you have a plan?"

But Erindil was already at her shelves, his long fingers dancing over the dark glass bottles, reading the peeling paper labels. "Wormwood, yes, yes, we'll need that. Blessed thistle, absolutely essential. Salamander toes!" He paused, holding up a jar with something floating in murky liquid. "Goodness, I hope we won't need those."

Iris disappeared into the back room while Erindil continued his whirlwind inventory, piling bottles and jars in his arms. When she returned, she carried two cups of steaming tea, pressing one into Vaskel's hands before sipping her own.

They stood together, watching the elf work and mutter continuously in what might have been Elvish or might have been nonsense.

"Dragon scales, no, too potent. Moonflower petals, yes, but only if harvested during a new moon. Do you know when they were plucked? No? Pity. We'll make do with morning glory, though it's really not the same thing at all..."

Vaskel's tea sat untouched in his hands, growing cold as Erindil assembled an impressive array of ingredients on the counter.

Finally, the elf stopped, placing his hands on his hips and surveying his collection with satisfaction. Only then did he seem to notice his audience. "Is that tea? Perfect! I'm absolutely parched."

He plucked the untouched cup from Vaskel's hands and drained it in three long swallows, despite it most certainly being stone cold.

"What do we do next?" Vaskel asked once the elf had drunk his tea.

Erindil set down the empty cup and beamed at him. "Once we mix all this up properly—in a specific order, naturally—and simmer it for a day at precisely the right temperature, we only need to add hairs from both bound souls." He waved a hand airily. "Then poof! The potion is complete."

That didn't sound too bad. Getting a strand of Marina's hair shouldn't be impossible since she wore it loose.

Relief must have shown on his face because Erindil wagged a finger at him. "Gathering the hairs is the easy part, dear boy."

He spotted Iris's cup where she'd set in on the counter, picked it up and drained that too. "The tricky part is getting both bound souls to drink it."

"Should I assume it won't taste good?" Vaskel asked.

Erindil clasped his hands behind his back. "You should assume it will smell and taste rancid."

Vaskel's heart dropped to the vicinity of his boots. "Both of us have to drink it?"

"Naturally," Iris muttered as she gave him a sympathetic look.

Get Marina to drink a potion? Marina, who trusted no one and suspected everything, would as soon down a malodorous potion as she'd sprout pixie wings.

Vaskel needed a backup plan—and fast.

Twenty-Seven

VASKEL AND IRIS appraised the mess that covered the countertop of the apothecary shop as the bell over the door still echoed its ring from Erindil's departure. The elf had swept out with as much gusto as he'd entered, unfortunately leaving the detritus of his potion-making behind.

The cauldron was simmering in the back of the shop on the hot plate Iris typically used for her teakettle, the unusual ingredients waiting for one remaining hair to be added.

"I don't think he's used to cleaning up after himself," Vaskel said, carefully recapping a bottle of something labeled 'Essence of Nightshade - DO NOT INGEST' in Iris's spidery handwriting.

Iris laughed, the sound bright in the hushed shop. "When you travel with a full staff, a personal lute player, and a battle ostrich, I imagine mundane tasks like putting lids back on jars become rather foreign."

They worked in a comfortable rhythm, Vaskel's height useful for returning bottles to the highest shelves, while Iris sorted through the scattered herbs. He knew he should return to the tavern, but he found himself reluctant to leave the peace of the shop and the soothing presence of the apothecary.

"Thank you." Iris swept crushed lavender into her palm. "For helping with all this. I know you have work and worries enough."

He paused, holding a jar of what looked like pickled eyeballs. "After everything you've done for me? This is the least I could do."

Iris's smile was warm and soft, nothing like Marina's practiced sultry grin. He forced himself to look away before he got lost in it. "Sometimes it's hard to believe that Lira and Erindil are related."

Iris laughed. "Agreed. Thankfully, she didn't inherit Erindil's flair for the dramatic. She's much more like her gran—practical and determined. "

Vaskel knew that Iris and Lira's gran had been close friends, had run together in their younger days on adventures that were only hinted at in conversations. But the details had always remained vague. Now, with his own past adventures creating such current troubles, he found himself curious about theirs.

"What was she like?" he asked, settling a collection of small vials into their proper rack. "Lira's gran? And what were your adventures like?"

Iris's face softened with memory, her hands stilling on the herbs she was sorting. "Elia was brilliant. A whiz at potions—she could brew things I'd never even heard of. Once, she created a masking potion on the spot using only roadside weeds, a scant few drops of fish eye oil, and rainwater. It got us past a sleeping troll without it catching our scent." She chuckled at the memory. "Of course, it also made us smell like rotting fish for three days afterward. Being chased by a troll might have been better, now that I think about it."

Vaskel laughed at this.

"And there was the time at Blackstone Fortress," Iris continued, warming to her storytelling. "We were escaping with—well, that's not important—but a pack of direwolves was hunting us. Massive beasts, each one the size of a pony. We reached the gates just as they appeared on the horizon, but the lock was one of those dwarven puzzles, all gears and tumblers."

She mimed picking a lock, her fingers dancing in the air from muscle memory. "I had maybe thirty seconds before they reached us. My hands were shaking, and I could hear them howling, getting closer. Elia stood behind me, absolutely calm, counting down the seconds like she was timing tea. 'Twenty seconds, Iris. Fifteen. You've got this. Ten.' I got it open with three seconds to spare. We got through those gates and closed them behind us just as the first wolf slammed into them."

She breathed a sigh, the memory clearly a treasured one. But Vaskel couldn't help thinking of his own adventures, and the choices made in youth that now haunted his every step.

"Did you ever do anything you regret now?" he asked quietly. "Things that seemed right at the time but..."

Iris considered this, her fingers absently arranging dried flowers into neat piles. "There were moments, certainly. Times when the easier path called to us, when taking something that wasn't quite ours would have solved our problems, when using our skills for less noble purposes would have paid better." She met his eyes, her gaze steady and understanding. "But Elia and I kept each other accountable. When one of us felt tempted to stray from what was right, the other would pull them back. We were each other's compass."

"You miss her." It was a statement, not a question. Lira's gran and Iris' best friend had been gone for many years, but the loss was still evident in Iris's green eyes.

"I do. Losing her was so painful that I pulled away from people for a long time. I didn't want to get close to anyone because it hurt too much to lose them." The apothecary's pained expression turned soft. "I don't feel that way anymore."

Vaskel pulse quickened. He wanted to be the one that Iris got close to again after so long, but how could he risk her heart being shattered again with Marina's threat hanging over him?

"Your friendship sounds incredible," he said, deftly steering the conversation away from himself. "I wish I'd had that when I was younger. Someone to stop me before I made the kind of mistakes that follow you forever. Then I wouldn't be in this mess."

Iris moved closer, resting her hand on his arm. The touch was gentle but grounding, warm through his sleeve. "But you have it now," she said tenderly, her green eyes holding his with an intensity that made his breath catch. "You have Lira, and Sass, and all of us. It's never too late to right a wrong, Vaskel. It's never too late to choose a better path."

Something shifted in the air between them. The morning sun slanted through the shop windows, turning the dust motes to gold and casting a warm glow across Iris's face. Her hand was still on his arm, and he was acutely aware of how close she stood, close enough that he could see the flecks of gold in her green eyes, smell the bergamot oil that seemed to cling to her skin.

She tilted her face up toward his, and he leaned down, drawn to the brilliant, kind woman who'd spent sleepless nights trying to save him, who saw him not as a charming hellkin with a past but simply as Vaskel.

Their faces were inches apart. He could feel her breath, see her eyes flutter closed. Just a little closer and—

Marina's face flashed through his mind, a cold slap of a reminder that he was bound to another, his very soul claimed. How could he do this to Iris? How could he let her think there could be something between them when he might be gone tomor-row, dragged away by a bond he couldn't break? It wasn't fair to play with her heart when he wasn't free to give his own.

He pulled back abruptly, stepping away so quickly that he nearly knocked over a black glass bottle of elderflower extract.

"I'm sorry," he said, his voice rough. "I should go."

Confusion flashed across Iris's face, followed by something that looked heartbreakingly like hurt. "Vaskel—"

He was already backing toward the door. "Thank you for—for everything, but I shouldn't take up any more of your time."

He fled before she could respond, the bell above the door ringing his retreat. The cold air outside slammed into him, but it wasn't enough to erase the warmth of where her hand had touched his arm or the look in her eyes just before he'd pulled away.

Vaskel trudged back through the village, his boots heavy on the frozen ground. The marks on his arms burned, but it was nothing compared to the ache in his chest. He'd hurt Iris. He'd seen the confusion in her eyes.

The soul bind felt heavier than ever, not just because of the marks spreading across his skin but because of what it was costing him. Not only his freedom, but the chance at something real, something good, something he hadn't even realized he wanted until it was impossible to have.

When he glanced up, he glimpsed Erindil hurrying over the bridge toward the castle. Why was the elf heading there, and why was he in an entirely different outfit than he'd been wearing earlier? Vaskel knew Erindil had *not* been wearing a simple dark cloak. Did the elf even own a garment that wasn't trimmed in fur or gilded fringe?

Unfortunately, he was so distracted by spotting Erindil that he didn't see the hand reach for him through the shop door, closing tightly around his arm.

Twenty-Eight

"I'M SO glad I spotted you!" Pip tugged him inside the bakery with surprising strength. "I need your opinion."

Vaskel dropped the arm he'd cocked to defend himself as he allowed himself to be led into the bakery. He supposed he had time for a friend, and there was no doubt he could use the mood boost of baked goods.

"It's a new creation inspired by one of the flavors I'm considering for Lira's wedding cake. Sweet cherry nestled in buttery pastry with a sugar glaze—but I've made two versions and can't decide!"

Pip thrust two pastries into his hands. Like all the halfling's creations, they smelled intoxicating and looked delicious. Golden pastry was folded into delicate roses around dark red cherry filling; one was drizzled with plain sugar glaze as white and glistening as fresh snow and the other was crowned with a ribbon of dark chocolate.

"Try them!" Pip bounced on his toes and rubbed his plump hands together, his hair abristle.

Vaskel bit into the plain glazed one first. The pastry was buttery and light, giving way to tart-sweet cherries that burst on his tongue. He licked at the sugar glaze that stuck to his lips, nearly moaning with pleasure. Then he tried the second version, which was richer and more decadent, the bite of dark chocolate cutting the sweetness of the cherries.

"They're both delicious," he said honestly, "I couldn't pick a favorite."

The halfling clapped his hands, flour puffing into the air. "Wonderful! I'll make both! Oh, I must get back to the ovens—the next batch should be ready!"

He scurried toward the back of the bakery, leaving Vaskel holding the half-eaten pastries and marveling how Pip's enthusiasm had dragged him from his dark mood.

Then the bakery door swung open. Freezing air swooped in, carrying snowflakes and a presence that made every muscle in Vaskel's body go rigid.

Marina swept in like an icy gust, and before he could step back, she'd looped her arm through his, her touch burning even through his sleeve.

"Vaskel," she purred. "You've been avoiding me. I'm starting to think you don't enjoy my company anymore."

He tried to pull away without making it obvious, acutely aware of Pip watching them from behind the counter. The last thing he needed was to cause a scene in the halfling's bakery, unless he was ready to reveal why he disliked Marina. But that would mean revealing his dark past, and Vaskel couldn't imagine his new friends discovering he'd been part of a murderous crew and still smiling at him the same way.

"I've been busy," he managed through gritted teeth.

"Of course you have." She turned that devastating smile on Pip, who'd turned at the sound of the door. "And who is this delightful creature?" She fluttered long red fingers at the pastries behind glass. "The creator of these stunning treats, I take it."

Pip practically beamed at the compliment. "Pip Brambleheart, at your service! Are you a friend of Vaskel's?"

"Oh yes," Marina said, squeezing Vaskel's arm hard enough to make the marks flare with pain. "We go way back. Practically family, you might say."

"Any friend of Vaskel's is a friend of mine!" Pip exclaimed, already reaching for a pastry. "You must try my newest creation—my treat."

Marina accepted the cheery pastry, taking a delicate bite and closing her eyes in apparent rapture. "You're a true artist, Master Brambleheart."

Pip smiled brighter as he launched into chatter about cherries. Marina listened with rapt attention, one of her many techniques for charming strangers and winning their trust.

Vaskel used this distraction to slip free from Marina's grip, darting out the door while Pip handed her a crusty morning roll. But he'd barely made it three steps before he walked straight into another hellkin. It was the one he'd seen watching him in the market.

Before he could walk away, fingers like iron closed around his arm, yanking him to a stop. Marina had moved with the unnatural stealth she'd always possessed, catching him before he could get far.

"That was rude," she said, her voice still pleasant but her grip bruising. "Here I am, trying to get to know your charming new friends, and you run from me like I'm the enemy."

"It's me you want," he snarled, no longer caring about maintaining appearances or about the young hellkin taking a menacing step toward him. "Leave them alone. Leave Thrain alone."

Her smile sharpened into something predatory, and she shared a knowing smile with the other hellkin. "Time is running out, Vaskel. For you, certainly, but especially for your dwarf friend. He's quite taken with the idea of adventure, and me, of course." She leaned closer, her breath hot against his ear. "He'd make such an excellent addition to my crew. All that passion and that desperate need to make his mark. He reminds me of a young hellkin I once knew."

Rage boiled in his chest. "Leave. Him. Alone."

Marina pulled back, studying his face with mock sympathy. "If you behave, if you come willingly when I call, then you have nothing to worry about. Neither does Thrain." She slid her gaze to the young hellkin. "Karv would prefer not to crew with a dwarf, isn't that right?"

The hellkin—presumably Karv—grunted and bared his teeth.

Marina's fingers traced along Vaskel's shirtsleeve and over the unseen marks. "But if you don't come willingly..." She shrugged languidly. "Well, you do have such delightful friends."

She released him abruptly, causing him to stumble. With perfect composure, she adjusted her cloak.

"The three days are quickly coming to an end, Vaskel. I told you I've missed you, and that was the truth. I grow impatient of waiting for you to join my crew, so we can go back to the way we were together." She released a sigh that seemed laden with nostalgia. "The choice is yours, just as it always has been. Come willingly and fulfill the promise you willingly made, or I'll take what's mine anyway, along with anyone else who catches my fancy."

Then she spun on one heel, while Karv stared at Vaskel for another few moments, his glare making it perfectly clear what he thought of Vaskel joining their crew. As Marina sauntered away with her hips swaying, and Karv finally followed her, Vaskel watched them go with fury burning through his veins like acid. His hands clenched into fists, the marks on his arms feeling like brands, like chains, like failure.

How did Marina not see that he wasn't the hellkin he'd been? It was true that he'd once wanted to be like her, but that was so long ago it was hard to imagine himself so empty and power-hungry. A small part of him almost felt pity that she was desperate for someone who no longer existed.

He stumbled the rest of the way to the tavern, hesitating outside the door to the Tusk & Tail and bracing one hand on the rough stone. Despite Marina's threats echoing in his head, they were not what haunted him. It was Iris's green eyes glistening with hurt that mocked him. It was the moment he'd almost been brave enough to reach for happiness that tormented him. Not that he deserved happiness or Iris. Not after the things he'd done.

The marks of the soul bind prickled again, reminding him of Marina's deadline and the dark fate marching toward him.

He felt more cursed than ever.

Twenty-Nine

WHEN VASKEL WALKED BACK into the tavern, Sass had roused herself from bed and was busily stoking a fresh fire, although Val was nowhere to be seen.

"She went home," Sass said before he could ask. "And don't think I didn't see you sneaking a peek at us this morning."

"I wasn't sneaking a peek," Vaskel grumbled, his mind still consumed with dark thoughts. "I was looking for Thrain."

"Aye, well." Sass eyed him as she straightened and let the

kindling catch beneath the pile of peat. "I heard him come in, but he's gone now."

Vaskel grunted. "I tried to talk to him, but he's too taken in by Marina. He believes her story of being a healer who's come to help the old laird."

Sass reared back, hands planted firmly on her hips. "That woman a healer?" She shook her head. "Thrain has always been a fool when it comes to womenfolk. I suppose some things never change."

Vaskel hoped that wasn't true. He hoped he'd changed, although at this point he didn't know if that made any difference.

Clattering in the kitchen drew his attention, and he hiked a thumb toward the swinging half doors. "Is Lira's baking going better today?"

Sass bobbled her head, and the dark braid she'd twisted into a bun bobbled. "I haven't heard any crashes, so I'm taking that as a good sign."

Vaskel headed for the kitchen with Sass close at his heels. When he pushed through the doors, he was pleased to see Lira humming as she mixed ingredients in a large ceramic bowl. Crumpet perched on his hind legs on the large wooden worktable that centered the room, holding a wooden spoon while Bramble was using his tiny hands to peel a lemon.

She looked up and grinned. "Top of the morning!"

Vaskel darted a questioning glance at Sass, who looked equally confused. "You're in a good mood this morning."

"After talking with Korl, I have a whole new outlook on the wedding." She paused in her stirring. "If Pip wants to bake a five-tier cake, why should I mind? Especially if Sass and Thrain each want to claim an entire tier."

Sass mumbled something about maybe not eating the whole tier herself.

"And Glen as a ring bearer will be something people will talk about for ages," Lira continued. "What bride doesn't want a memorable wedding?"

Vaskel bit back the urge to say that, considering his behavior during the Solstice Festival, Glen's presence might not be memorable in the way she'd want.

Lira squared her shoulders and released a breath. "Besides, I'm lucky to have so many friends who care about me and Korl. I'm focusing on being grateful for that and not fretting about the details."

Vaskel wondered if maybe she and Korl rushing out of the tavern to their flat above the tinker's shop played a part in her sunny disposition, but he kept quiet about that.

Sass gave her friend a knowing look. "Can you put a pin in your gratitude long enough for us to talk about Vaskel's problem?"

Lira shot the hellkin a questioning glance, and he shrugged. "I told her and Val. I felt I owed it to them now that Thrain's been pulled into the mess."

Lira's face tightened with concern, but Vaskel continued before she could speak. "The good news is Erindil remembered dealing with a soul bind centuries ago. He's concocted a potion that might break it."

"That's wonderful!" Her face brightened immediately.

"It takes a day to simmer properly," he cautioned. "Plus, I need to procure one of Marina's hairs to add to it."

Sass drew herself up to her full height. "Snatch a hair from that hellkin's head? Leave that to me."

Vaskel had no problem imagining Sass yanking a hair from Marina's head as she worked her way through the great room.

"But here's the real problem," he said, "both of us have to consume it. And, according to Erindil, it will taste foul."

"How will we manage that?" Lira's brow furrowed as she considered the challenge. "Marina seems too clever to be tricked into chugging some mysterious potion."

Vaskel shook his head. They were so close to a solution, but this last obstacle seemed significant.

"We could knock her out and force it down her throat," Sass said, her voice menacing as she pounded a fist into her palm.

Sneaking up on the hellkin to knock her out would be as tricky as convincing her to drink a potion. "Let's call that our backup plan."

Sass shrugged. "What about slipping it into some ale?"

Vaskel considered this. "If it's truly foul, she'd detect it in one sip. From what Erindil said, she needs to drink more than that."

Lira squeezed his arm, her touch grounding him. "Don't worry, Vask. We've come up with crazy plans before, remember? Remember the time we infiltrated a laird's party dressed as minstrels? We'll figure this out too."

With that, she spun around and opened the oven door, releasing a cloud of fragrant steam.

Sass sucked in a greedy breath. "What are those? They aren't scones."

Lira used one of the orange pot holders Val had knitted her to remove a metal tray dotted with dark brown, knobby mounds topped with gooey, white puffs. "I found the recipe for these cookies in Gran's book, and I think it's perfect for the cold weather."

She placed the tray on the table and drizzled melted chocolate on top of each cookie from a small saucepan. The air smelled of something rich and sweet and, dare Vaskel say, seductive.

Lira used a flat metal utensil to slide two of the rounds onto a plate, then she extended it to Vaskel and Sass. "You're my first taste-testers."

Vaskel took one, holding it gingerly by the hot edges and blowing on it before taking a bite. The moment he bit into it, flavors exploded across his tongue—plenty of sweetness but also decadent chocolate. It was like drinking hot cocoa while sitting by a roaring fire, all condensed into cookie form.

He groaned with pleasure, the sound entirely undignified but completely genuine.

"Gran called it a hot cocoa cookie," Lira said. "The recipe was tucked between one for butter cake and instructions for enchanting doorways."

"It's very rich," Sass mumbled through her mouthful, "but that's a good thing."

As Vaskel chewed the decadent cookie, savoring every sticky morsel, his mind spinning. It was rich and filled with intense flavor. Maybe it was just rich enough to mask the flavor of a potion.

Vaskel reached for another cookie straight off the pan, holding it up. "Maybe we don't have to get Marina to drink the potion. Maybe we can get her to eat it."

Thirty

"SO LET ME GET THIS STRAIGHT," Sass said from where she swung her legs on the stool. "The plan is for me to snatch a hair from the hellkin's head that will go in the potion that Iris is brewing in her back room. Then when that's done brewing, Lira will bake it into some cookies that both you and Marina will need to eat."

Now that he heard the plan out loud, Vaskel didn't feel like it was so simple.

"If we don't want her to suspect anything, I might need to add something to the cookies." Lira tapped a finger on her chin. "Something else to mask the flavor."

"Dwarven food uses a lot of garlic," Sass said.

"In cookies?" Lira wrinkled her nose.

Sass twitched one shoulder. "In everything really."

"Another reason you never hear of great chefs being dwarves," Lira said under her breath.

"Heard that!" Sass slid off her stool and landed on the wooden floor with a thud.

"I was thinking about something sweeter but with enough of a kick to hide any noxious flavor." Lira turned to her shelves and scanned her stores of ingredients. "Maybe spiced rum."

Vaskel snapped his fingers. "I've got it."

Both women turned to him.

"Rosie's apple brandy, of course," he said.

Lira pulled him into a quick embrace and gave him a hard kiss on the cheek. "Vask, you're a genius. Rosie's apple brandy could strip paint off a wagon. It will be the perfect way to mask the potion."

"It will ruin your cookies, though," he said, which was truly a shame since the hot cocoa cookies were perfect.

Lira brushed aside his worry with a flick of her hand. "I'll make a new recipe just for Marina." She grinned at him. "But I'll make it delicious since you'll have to eat it too."

She turned to her two woodland assistants and clapped her hands. "Okay, boys, new task. We have to find the perfect ingredients to go in a chocolate brandy cookie."

Bramble headed for the open window while Crumpet flew to eye the highest shelves.

"We have a day to perfect it," Vaskel reminded them before pivoting to Sass. "But less time to get Marina's hair."

"Don't you worry your pretty, red head about it." Sass patted him roughly on the arm as she turned toward the door. "I've got it well in hand."

Pretty, red head? Vaskel mouthed to Lira as Sass strode from the kitchen.

Lira giggled and shrugged as Vaskel called after Sass. "I thought you were going to get it from her tonight."

He followed Sass into the great room, which was still blessedly empty aside from the crackling fire. "I doubt she'll be here until Thrain brings her in tonight."

Sass rolled her eyes. "I'm not waiting for that when the clock is ticking." She untied her apron and tossed it onto the bar top. "I'll be back soon."

"Wait!" Vaskel chased after her as she took quick steps toward the door. "You're going to find Marina?"

She pushed through the front door. "That's right. How hard can it be to find the only female hellkin currently in Wayside?"

"Is your plan to walk up to her and yank a hair from her head without her noticing?"

Sass paused once they were outside. "I haven't finalized my plan yet. Sometimes the best tunnels are the ones you didn't set out to dig." She held up a chubby finger. "But never underestimate a dwarf."

Vaskel stared as she walked off, arms swinging. He wasn't sure if he understood all her dwarf mining wisdom, but if he'd learned one thing since befriending dwarves, it was not to underestimate them—or try to out-drink them.

Thirty-One

"WHERE'S SASS?" Lira pushed through the swinging kitchen doors then paused when she only found Vaskel in the tavern's great room.

He ran a hand through his long hair, his fingertips brushing his horns. "She's run off to find Marina and get that hair."

Lira stopped wiping her hands on her dusty apron. "Now? I thought she was going to do that tonight when the hellkin came to the tavern."

"She said something about the clock ticking and not waiting." He shook his head. "You know how stubborn she is."

Lira muttered something about dwarves having hard heads before resting one hand on her hip. "How is she going to find Marina?"

"Again," Vaskel said, "you know Sass. She was too busy being determined to come up with a plan. Apparently, some of the best tunnels are the ones you never planned to dig."

Lira's brows lifted. "Now you're spouting dwarf mining wisdom?"

Vaskel held both palms up as if in surrender. "I'm only repeating what Sass said."

Lira let out a loud breath. "I don't like the thought of her barreling headlong into danger, and we both know that Sass isn't as subtle as she thinks she is."

"I'll go after her."

"Won't Marina spot you in a second?" Lira crossed her arms over her chest and eyed her friend. "Of anyone in Wayside, I think you have the least chance of sneaking up on the only other hellkin in the village."

Vaskel narrowed his eyes at her. "Then do you have any better suggestions?"

Lira gave him a curt nod as she untied her apron. "We'll go together. We've worked together enough that we know how to play roles and be stealthy. Besides, who would suspect two friends out for a walk?"

He flicked his gaze behind her. "What about your baking?"

"Crumpet and Bramble can handle it. Crumpet could whip up scones in his sleep, and Bramble has become quite the assistant."

She poked her head over the half-doors and give brief instructions to the pair of woodland creatures who were apparently going to man the kitchen while they followed Sass.

"Are you sure about this?" he asked once she'd rejoined him and tossed her apron onto the bar top.

"Absolutely." She took strides toward the door, leaving him to hurry to catch up. "I need a break from work anyway. The fresh air will do me good, help me clear my mind."

They exited the tavern, letting the door shut with a soft creak. There was no sign of Sass, which wasn't a shock. The dwarf might have short legs, but she could move quickly when she was on a mission. And she'd definitely been on a mission when she'd set out to find Marina.

"So, we're searching for a dwarf who's searching for a hellkin," Lira said as she swung her head from side to side.

"Who's staying at the castle pretending to be a healer."

"The castle?" Lira bristled, knowing just as well as Vaskel what was hidden in the dungeons. "And the laird at Grayhelm believes her?"

"Marina is very convincing," Vaskel said. "All hellkins are skilled in charm and cunning, but she's a master at her craft. I've seen her charm the pants right off a man—literally. We left him pants-less on the side of the road as Marina took his horse and all his coin."

"Charming." Lira pivoted so she could eye the top of the stone castle peeking over the tree line. "Does Sass know this?"

"Yes to Marina staying at the castle, but no to the pants-stealing story."

Lira's lips twitched. "Then I say we make a quick pass through the village, then head to the castle. If we get lucky, Sass hasn't gotten too far."

The two friends fell in step as they walked down the snowy road toward the village proper, passing Rog's and Rosie's wooden wagon with faded apples adorning the sides. When they reached the intersection with the stone bridge leading to the castle in one direction and the shops in the other, Lira took a deep breath and sighed.

"I know it's a small place and there's nothing particularly special about it, but I love this little village."

He whirled on her. "What do you mean there's nothing particularly special about Wayside?"

She shrugged, her cheeks flushed from the cold and perhaps embarrassment. "It's a village like any other. There's a tavern and a bakery, a blacksmith and a chandler."

He shook his head. "But the tavern is the one you and Sass brought back to life, and the baker makes the best sweet rolls I've ever tasted. It isn't the shops or the buildings that make Wayside so special, it's the people."

"You're right." She gave him a shy smile. "I honestly didn't know if I'd ever find a place like this, a place where I belong. Even though this is where I grew up, I didn't know if it would become my home when I returned."

"But you did. You found what you were always searching for, Lira. A home. A place to belong. People who love you not for what you can steal or how well you can fight, but just for being you."

She nudged him with her elbow, a gesture so familiar it made his chest ache. "You found it too, you know. This is your home now, as much as it is mine."

He swallowed hard around the lump that had suddenly formed in his throat. "That's what terrifies me."

She waited, knowing him well enough not to push.

"I fear losing it," he continued, his voice barely above a whisper. "This place, these people who've become family. I'm heartbroken at the thought of having to leave all of this. But I'm more afraid of putting the family I've found here in danger. Marina doesn't make idle threats, and if she brings her crew here—"

"We won't let that happen," Lira said firmly, taking his hand in hers. "None of us will let some uppity hellkin hurt someone we love."

A watery laugh escaped Vaskel's lips. "I hope Marina is the uppity hellkin in question."

Lira winked at him. "For now, she is."

From the corner of his eye, Vaskel spotted movement beyond the bridge. "There." He inclined his head as the edge of a cloak disappeared into the woods surrounding Grayhelm. "Someone is on their way to the castle."

"Sass?" Lira asked as she turned to follow Vaskel's gaze.

"Not sure," he admitted. "But someone in a hurry."

Lira gave him a grin he'd seen many times during their crewing days. "Then let's find out who."

Thirty-Two

VASKEL AND LIRA walked briskly but quietly across the icy stone bridge, placing each foot with care to avoid both slipping and making noise. Below, the stream gurgled and rushed, swollen with snowmelt and churning with bits of ice loosened from the banks.

By the time they reached the far side of the bridge, the mysterious figure was completely out of sight, but the open road was empty and the only other option was the path leading to the castle.

Without discussion, he and Lira took the road to Grayhelm.

The old laird had been sick for ages now, and it was hardly a secret. The castle's reduced guard, the hush that had settled over the formerly bustling fortress, and the way the grounds had withered were all signs of a lord too ill to rule properly.

But there was something else in that castle, something that iced Vaskel's blood—a dark mage imprisoned in the dungeons below, the one who'd nearly killed him and his friends before being captured, the one who'd been locked away for many moons now, supposedly rendered harmless by magic-suppressing chains. There was no chance Marina would have any connection to him or even knowledge of his existence. Was there?

Dread sent a chill through him colder than any winter gust as he passed through the stone archway into the castle yard. The change from the days long ago when he'd passed through the area and stopped at the castle was noticeable. Where once the courtyard had bustled with servants, merchants, and guards, now it stood nearly empty. It was less dilapidated than quiet. The castle felt like a place holding its breath, waiting for death.

A few guards patrolled, but it was clear they had grown unused to frequent visitors. The only reason Vaskel didn't worry that the imprisoned mage was at risk of escaping was the fact that both Val and Korl checked on his security every time they were on patrol.

One guard noticed them and straightened slightly, though his hand didn't go to his weapon. "You have business here?"

Lira was already moving like she was a rogue and not a tavern baker. "We're looking for some friends of ours."

"Dwarves," Vaskel added.

The guard scratched his head. "You've lost some dwarves?" He glanced at another guard across the way and cocked a brow, as if wondering if they should be worried about a dwarf invasion. "How many?"

"Two," Lira said, flashing her sweetest smile. "They're friends. Not armed."

The guard rocked back on his heels. "I saw a dwarf, but she

said she was with the healer." He cocked a thumb vaguely over his shoulder. "She went to deliver something to her room."

Vaskel stiffened but tried not to let his worry show on his face. Sass was sneaking into Marina's room? He was both impressed by the plan and terrified. If Marina caught her...

"Up here?" Lira asked, her voice light and conversational as she made for the arched doorway.

Vaskel hurried after her, holding his breath in anticipation of the guards stopping them. But they didn't, and soon he and Lira were through the doorway and hurrying up winding stone steps.

"You don't think Sass is really going to sneak into Marina's room, do you?" he whispered, the words bouncing off the stone and echoing back to him.

"You mean do I think she's headstrong enough?" Lira asked.

Vaskel grunted. He didn't need an answer to that question. Part of him was impressed that Sass had come up with the idea to infiltrate where the hellkin was staying and look for a hair there. It was certainly less risky than snatching a hair from Martina's head. He gulped. Unless she was caught.

They crested the staircase, emerging into a stone hallway draped with dusty tapestries and flickering wall sconces. Heavy wooden doors lined both sides of the hall, with no indication which one could be the hellkin's quarters. If this was even the right corridor.

Lira moved to one, examining the door handle and grinning. "No locks."

Small favors, though Vaskel, as he imagined startling the occupants of the rooms and hoping very much that none of them were armed—or were Marina.

"You take one side, and I'll take the other," Lira said, reminding him so much of the days when they'd run together that his chest squeezed.

Vaskel nodded without speaking, but as his hand closed around the first iron door handle, a door farther down the hall creaked open. He and Lira both went rigid, and Vaskel glanced at the open stairwell, gauging how fast they could dash to it.

Before he could dive for cover, Sass stepped into the hallway and her gaze snagged on her friends. "What are you doing here?"

"Looking for you," Lira hissed.

Sass held up her small hand where several jet black hairs dangled from her fingers. "I got them."

Lira waved her toward them. "Good. Let's go before we're spotted."

Sass rushed down the corridor, her feet tapping on the stone floor, then the three of them went down the coiling steps single file until they reached the archway leading to the courtyard.

"You didn't happen to see Thrain, did you?" Vaskel asked before they stepped into the courtyard.

"He's not here," Sass said, her voice clipped. There was something she wasn't saying.

Lira stopped and turned, causing them all to bump into each other. "How are you so sure?"

"Because I saw Marina." Sass's expression hardened. "She's with someone new."

Vaskel's stomach dropped. He knew without even hearing a name that he wasn't going to like it. "Who?"

Thirty-Three

THE MARKS on Vaskel's arm prickled with unwanted heat as Marina stepped into the courtyard from another castle archway. It was as if they'd sensed her presence, the heat scorching beneath his flesh.

Lira sucked in a quick breath in front of them, but Marina was laughing too loudly for her to hear, the husky sound reverberating in the courtyard. It was only when the person Marina was laughing with came into view that Lira went rigid.

"Cali?" Vaskel husked, low enough that only Lira and Sass heard him.

"I'd be happy to teach you to shoot," Cali said as she strode into the open space next to Marina. She wore her usual snug pants and vest, leaving her gray-striped arms exposed.

"You're too generous." Marina leaned into the pantheri, resting a hand on her arm.

Even from where they were hiding in the shadows of the stairwell, Vaskel could see Cali's whiskers twitch with pleasure. He knew the archer well enough to know when she was truly pleased, although he hated seeing her smile bestowed on Marina.

Sass lurched forward, but Vaskel snagged her by the arm. "Don't. Don't let Marina see your outrage. She feeds on it."

Sass bared her teeth, but she didn't struggle against him. The three watched Marina and Cali walk across the courtyard and exit to the castle grounds, presumably so Cali could teach the hellkin to shoot arrows.

Of course, Vaskel knew Marina didn't need archery lessons. True, she wasn't the expert that Cali was, but she was close.

A growl rumbled deep in his throat once the hellkin and pantheri were out of sight. "We should go."

"We can't just leave Cali," Lira protested.

"I'm with Lira." Sass crossed her arms over her chest. "We have to get her away from that she-demon." She tipped her head to Vaskel. "No offense, Vask."

"None taken. Marina is the worst kind of infernal creature, but the best way we can help Cali is to work on ridding Wayside of her entirely."

Lira and Sass exchanged a wary look then Sass sighed. "He's right. There was no talking to Thrain while he was under Marina's spell, and I suspect it will be the same with Cali."

Lira released a begrudging sigh. "She seemed unusually attentive to Marina."

Vaskel grunted. "That's her talent, and the more she sees that her affections are causing distress to others, the more she tightens her hold."

Sass muttered some dark curses that even Vaskel had never heard, then she held up the long black hairs clutched in one fist. "At least I got the hairs for the potion. I suppose we should focus on that."

"And I'll focus on creating a recipe punchy enough to hide the flavor," Lira said with a determined nod as she headed across the courtyard and away from the castle.

Once they'd walked under the rusty portcullis, Vaskel craned his neck to look back at the ancient stone fortress. "At least Marina is distracted by trying to charm my friends."

"And that's a good thing?" Sass asked, huffing as she took two steps for every one of his as they continued down the wooded road toward the stone bridge.

Vaskel slowed his pace as they crossed the icy bridge. "It is when you consider it could be much worse."

Lira cast him a sidelong glance. "You mean...?"

"I mean that we'd be in much deeper trouble if she knew what was being held in the dungeons."

Even Sass's brown skin paled a shade or two as they all exchanged knowing looks. A dark mage was the last thing you wanted teamed up with a hellkin.

They walked past the wooden wagon where Rog and Rosie lived, and Sass snuck a glance behind them, as if Marina might hear them. "You're sure she doesn't know?"

Vaskel had considered this, but if Marina was busying herself with targeting his friends, she wasn't aware of the much more powerful weapon locked up in an iron cell. "If she did, she wouldn't bother with Thrain or Cali. If she knew the dark magic she could access, I doubt she'd even bother with me."

"That's both a comforting and terrifying thought," mumbled Lira as they approached the Tusk & Tail, the wooden sign swinging gently over the door.

Vaskel pushed it open, held it for his friends, and then followed them inside the warm great room, which was blessedly still standing.

"There you are!" A resounding belch followed the booming voice.

Vaskel spotted the top of Thrain's head behind the bar with a bottle of Rosie's brandy in each hand.

"Thrain?" Sass crossed the room quickly, snatched him by one ear and dragged him from behind the bar.

"Hells and cinders, woman!"

"What are you doing?" She asked when she finally released his ear. "It's barely noon and you're already drinking?"

Vaskel suspected he was drinking his woes away if Marina had thrown him over for Cali.

"'S nothing," the dwarf slurred. "Just some liquid courage."

"Before lunch?" Sass pressed, tapping one toe viciously on the wooden floor.

"Before I go fight for Marina." Train thrust out his barrel chest. "Before I challenge Cali to a duel."

Lira put a hand over her eyes and groaned. "Sweet, simmering cauldrons."

Thirty-Four

"THERE'S NOT GOING to be a duel," Sass announced, her eyes narrowed. "Cali is your friend, or have you forgotten that you thickheaded lug?"

Thrain frowned, and his shoulders sagged along with his whiskers. "I suppose she is that." He hiccuped loudly. "But how can I compete with a pantheri?"

"Maybe by not fighting over some total stranger," Lira said before she disappeared into the kitchen.

"Marina isn't a stranger!" Thrain bellowed, then belched again. "She's a goddess."

Vaskel reared back from the scent of apple brandy belch, waving a hand in front of his own face. As much as he wanted to shake the dwarf, he couldn't fault him for falling for such a skilled charmer. Not when he'd also believed her carefully crafted web of lies. Not when his soul was bound to hers because he'd trusted in her intoxicating promises.

Sass shot him a look that landed somewhere between pleading and exasperated. "You want to take this one?"

Vaskel hooked a hand under Thrain's elbow and steered him to the pair of overstuffed armchairs flanking the fire. He deposited the dwarf in Val's usual chair, and Thrain collapsed into it like a deflated wineskin.

Vaskel took the chair across from him, draping his tail over one armrest and hunching forward with his elbows on his knees. "Do you know how Marina told you we knew each other from way back, that we were childhood friends?"

Thrain scrunched his mouth as he focused on the hellkin, tilting his head and eyeing him warily. "But nothing more than friends, eh?"

Vaskel thought about how he'd felt about the female hellkin when he'd first met her. He'd been captivated by her beauty and her talent, marveling at how she sweet-talked her way into the good graces of others and out of all sorts of trouble. It had only been when he'd known her better that he'd seen the cracks in her facade and the malevolence beneath the seduction.

He took a deep breath. "We weren't childhood friends. We crewed together a long time ago."

The dwarf's brow furrowed. "That's not what—"

"I know what Marina said, but she was counting on me not wanting to reveal my past. She was right. I haven't wanted to admit that I ran with her and a few other dodgy types when I was a young hellkin because the things we did weren't honorable and I've been running from them ever since."

Just then, Lira emerged from the kitchen carrying two steaming ceramic mugs. She crossed the room and pressed one into Thrain's meaty hands and passed the other to Vaskel. "Drink this. It might help clear your head."

Vaskel curled his hands around the warm mug and inhaled the spicy aroma of chai steam curling from the hot drink. If he was being honest, he might have preferred the same liquid courage Thrain had, but he sipped the chai, anyway.

Lira patted his shoulder before she returned to the kitchen, leaving the hellkin and dwarf alone in the great room. Vaskel didn't dwell too long on where Sass had gone, since he needed to focus on Thrain and stopping a duel.

Thrain slurped his chai loudly through his bristly beard. "You crewed with a healer?"

Vaskel bit back a scoffing laugh. "She wasn't a healer then, and she isn't now. Marina did what I did. She sensed danger and used her natural infernal charms to get what she needed from marks. She's also deadly with a blade and knows her way around a bow."

Thrain blinked as if the hellkin was speaking troll. "I don't understand."

"Hellkins are naturally gifted when it comes to manipulation and cunning. I've spent decades trying to use my talents for good, but it's all too easy to fall into the trap of using them for nefarious purposes."

The dwarf sat up straighter, bristling. "You're saying Marina, my Marina is nefar...lious?"

"I'm telling you the truth, Thrain. She isn't who she claims to be."

Vaskel's friend sank back in his chair, sloshing a bit of chai onto his long whiskers. "But why? Why come here and pretend to be something she's not? It doesn't make sense."

The hellkin paused. If he told Thrain the truth, there would be no going back. The dwarf could decide not to believe him. He could run back to Marina and tell her what Vaskel had said. He could bring even more of her wrath onto him and possibly the village. Marina could very well forget about the three days she'd given him and insist his time was up.

In the past, he might have taken the safest route. He might not have dared to trust his friend. He might not have taken a chance that a fledgling friendship could be more powerful than the hellkin's dark influence. Even now, he hesitated before taking the leap.

Then he dragged in a deep breath and shoved up his shirt sleeve. "Because of this."

Thrain's gaze fell onto the inky marks weaving up his arm. "What in Grognick's beard is that?"

"This is the soul bind that Marina put on me twenty years ago when I was too young and foolish to know better. The reason she's here is that she's come to collect on it."

Thrain squinted so hard his eyes disappeared completely beneath his bushy eyebrows. "Collect on it?"

The marks sizzled with heat, and Vaskel scratched at them before pushing his sleeve over them again. "Make me go with her. Force me to return to crewing with her and a bunch of hellkins who don't care a whit about glory or honor."

Thrain drained his chai and scraped a hand through his unruly hair. "She did talk about moving on from Wayside. She said I could come with her. Said that a dwarf who's crewed before would be an asset. That's when I told her I'd never crewed before." His face twisted at the memory, and he let out a bitter laugh. "I told her I was good at tunnel work, and the only quest I'd been on was the one to find Sass."

Vaskel's gut twisted, knowing all too well where this was headed.

"I might have mentioned that you and Lira and Cali were the ones in Wayside who'd crewed together." Thrain sank deeper into the upholstered chair as if the truth was pressing down on him. "That's when she stopped suggesting I leave with her and told me she was busy when I went to find her in the castle. Then I saw her with Cali. I thought the archer was to blame but..." He looked up, his expression stricken. "Do you think she went after Cali? Is this my fault?"

Already, Vaskel's heart had started pounding as he thought about Marina's designs on Cali. Of course, the archer would be valuable to her new crew. He only hoped the pantheri wasn't as easily enchanted as Thrain, although he knew better than to underestimate Marina.

Vaskel shook his head. "None of this is on you, Thrain. You had no way of knowing."

Because I was too afraid to reveal my own dark past to warn anyone.

He shook off this thought. At least he was being honest now.

The tavern door swung open, and Sass walked in along with a gust of frigid air.

Thrain gave his head a shake. "Where'd you go?"

"I popped in to the apothecary's." Sass gave Vaskel a pointed look, which meant she'd taken Marina's hairs to Iris.

He exhaled and inclined his head to her. At least they were one step closer to breaking the bind, even if it felt like he was running out of time.

"Any luck?" Sass motioned to Thrain. "Or does he still think he stands a chance against Cali?"

"Hey!" Thrain bellowed, looking both affronted and chagrined. "I can wield an axe."

"Not before her arrow cuts you down," Sass said under her breath.

"Don't worry," Vaskel said. "I told him—everything."

Sass's eyes widened, but she took long steps toward Thrain, wagging a finger at him. "Now don't let me hear you running your mouth about this or telling it in one of your tall tales."

Thrain's mouth opened and then closed again, as if he wanted to take offense but ran out of steam. "Why would I want anyone to know I got taken in like this?" Thrain rubbed his forehead and groaned. "Is there such a thing as a morning hangover?"

Sass rolled her eyes, pulling him up and prodding him toward the stairs. "It's time for you to sleep this off."

Vaskel watched both dwarves head for the back staircase and the rooms above the tavern. It was time for him to think of a way to save Cali.

Thirty-Five

"YOU'RE BAKING?" Vaskel asked once he was inside Lira's kitchen. "Aren't you worried about Cali with Marina?"

"Of course, I am." Lira slid him a severe look as she stirred something dark in a small copper saucepan. "But you know baking calms me and helps me think."

Vaskel eyed her signature apple cider cake and the pans of cut-out scones waiting to go in the oven before breathing in the scent of fruit scones already baking. Crumpet was scooping flour from a burlap sack, and Bramble was washing ruby-red cranberries in a bowl of water. "If that's the case, then you must have come up with a hundred brilliant solutions already."

Lira made a face at him. "That's not how it works. I don't get more ideas the more things I bake. Sometimes the process takes a while."

A while was exactly what Vaskel did not have. But he tempered his impatience, reminding himself that he should be grateful that Lira was helping him with his problem. Considering he'd made this deal with Marina years before he'd even met Lira, he had no right to demand she drop everything to save him. But now it wasn't just him who needed saving.

"I'm not shocked Thrain fell for Marina's ways," Vaskel admitted. "But I didn't think she'd get to Cali."

Lira pressed her lips together as the contents of her pan bubbled, sending up clouds of sweet, fragrant steam. Then she looked up and met Vaskel's gaze. "Cali wants the same things all of us do. She wants to be valued and desired just as much as Thrain, even if she might seem less of a target."

Crumpet chattered something, and Lira hastened the pan off the heat. "You're right. I don't want to scorch the chocolate."

Vaskel tried not to be unsettled by Lira talking with an enchanted woodland creature. Besides, he'd seen more astonishing things over the years than a team of wee beasties, as Sass called them, working as kitchen assistants.

"Do you think Cali's been lonely?" Vaskel asked. "Do you think she was an easy mark for Marina because we've been too busy running the tavern to spend as much time with her?"

Lira swept the back of her hand across her forehead. "I honestly don't know. I do think we're assuming a lot. All we saw was Marina asking Cali to teach her to shoot a bow."

"Which she knows how to do," Vaskel added. "Quite well, I should say."

"So we know Marina was lying, and it's probably safe to say that her intentions aren't on the up and up, but we can't be sure Cali will fall for it like Thrain did."

"It's hard to imagine Cali being as lovesick as the dwarf."

Lira tapped her wooden spoon on the side of the pan, and melted chocolate oozed down it. "Have we ever seen Cali lovesick?"

Vaskel ran a hand down his short beard, thinking back to their crewing days. "There was that pretty librarian in Frostmoor. I always had a feeling they bonded over more than romance novels."

Lira smiled at the memory. "I forget her name, but she was nice. It was a shame we had to move on."

"We were always moving on back then."

Lira nodded. "None of us put down roots or made deep connections since we were always going from one bounty or quest to the next."

"Except for Rog. He always went home to Rosie."

Lira chuckled. "We just didn't know that that home was a brandy wagon."

Vaskel warmed at the thought of his gnome friend and his wife, happy that they'd ended up in Wayside with the rest of their crew. All except two, he reminded himself as the warm feeling faded.

"Speaking of..." Lira reached for a small jar of Rosie's apple brandy and removed the cork with a pop before glugging some into the melted chocolate.

Vaskel eyed the pan. "Are you making...? Is that...?"

"The recipe I want to add the potion to?" Lira met his gaze. "It is. I want to do a test run before we add the potion."

Vaskel nodded, his chest suddenly tight. Did his future really hinge on chocolate brandy cookies?

"This might be my fault," Lira said as she whisked the brandy into the chocolate.

Vaskel stared at her. "The soul bind? Marina?"

"No." She whisked faster. "Cali. I've been so distracted by the ridiculous wedding plans that I haven't been spending as much time with her."

He reached for her hand and stopped her whisking. "It's understandable. You also moved in with Korl and have been working at the tavern every day on top of having a wedding to plan."

Lira frowned. "Being a bride is no excuse for ignoring your friends."

"You've hardly been ignoring anyone." He squeezed her hand. "I promise."

She gave him a grateful smile. "Is to too late to elope?"

He laughed at this. "Don't ask me. Hellkins don't even bother with weddings."

Lira's grin faded. "Even if I haven't been the most attentive friend, I like to think that Cali is too clever to fall under Marina's spell. For all we know, she was merely being helpful."

Vaskel wanted to believe that, but he also knew just how cunning Marina could be, especially if she knew Cali was important to Vaskel and that she could be a valuable member of a crew. "There's one person who has been spending more time with Cali than any of us."

Lira leveled her dripping spoon at him. "Iris!"

"Cali is always in her back room borrowing books. Almost every time I pop in, she's there to talk about pirate romance or kraken romance or whatever it is she likes to read."

"Pirates," Lira said as Crumpet dumped a cup full of flour into the chocolate and brandy mixture. She cocked her head at the hellkin. "How often are you popping in to Iris's, Vask?"

Although his red skin couldn't flush, his face warmed. "No more than is normal."

Crumpet huffed out a breath and took the spoon from Lira, taking over mixing as she eyed Vaskel.

"Since I know that hellkins rarely get sick, is it normal for you to pop in to the apothecary's at all? It isn't like you're into reading pirate romance."

He spluttered, the words tripping over his tongue as he tried to explain himself. "Iris and I are friends just like she and Cali are friends, so it's perfectly normal for me to visit her."

This only seemed to widen Lira's smile. "Somehow I don't think it's the same as Iris and Cali's friendship, do you?"

He opened his mouth then clamped it shut, realizing too late that his tail was flicking nervously behind him. Lira knew him too well for him to get much past her, and her eyes went straight to his tail.

"I think I've been too distracted by the wedding to notice quite a few things," she said with a smug grin.

"We're talking about Cali," Vaskel reminded her, "and trying to make sure she doesn't get taken in by Marina."

Some of the smugness in Lira's smile vanished. "You're right. You're also right that Iris has been spending more time with her than anyone. If someone might know Cali's state of mind, it would be her."

Vaskel paused. "You don't think Cali would tell Marina what's in the castle dungeon, do you?"

Lira's oven-warmed cheeks paled. "Why would she? She wants Malek to stay locked away as much as we all do."

Vaskel nodded, wanting to believe her. Wanting to believe that Marina would never get that information from Cali.

"I can talk to Iris. I should check on the potion anyway," Vaskel said, changing the subject and taking care not to meet Lira's shrewd gaze. "I can tell her what we know about Cali and Marina and see what she thinks."

"I'll keep working on the cookies. If the potion is done later today, I'd like to get them made by this evening."

"Then all I have to do is convince Marina to eat one."

Lira opened the oven door, leaning back as steam billowed

from inside. She used her knitted oven mitts to retrieve two pans of golden-brown scones and set them on the wooden worktable. The potent aroma of cinnamon drenched the air, and even Vaskel's stomach growled.

"It will work, Vask," Lira said as she waved an oven mitt over the scones. "Who doesn't love baked goods?"

Thirty-Six

VASKEL HURRIED THROUGH THE VILLAGE, the sky leaden and warning of more snow. It was almost afternoon, which meant he didn't have time to spare. Soon folks would drift into the Tusk & Tail for scones and chai, and some would linger until dinner.

He kept his head down, even ignoring the punchy aroma of yeast soaking the air near Pip's bakery. As much as he wanted to stop in for a sweet treat or even a crusty roll, he needed to get to the apothecary.

Vaskel didn't bother to slow once he ducked under the black-and-white-striped awning, pushing open the door and letting the bell jangle as he burst inside. But there was no one behind the counter. No Iris tending to customers. No sound of her bustling around in the back.

For a moment, he stiffened, and the tip of his tail quivered. He hadn't sensed danger, but what if he was wrong? What if the soul bind and the marks burning their way up his arm had hampered his ability to detect threats? What if Marina was there? What if Cali had inadvertently brought the enemy into the very place where they were working to break her infernal magic?

Holding his breath, he walked as stealthily as possible toward the heavy brown curtains, his fingers hovering over the blade tucked in his belt. Just as he reached the velvet curtain, it flew back and a shriek rent the air.

"Hells and cinders, Vaskel!" Iris pressed a hand to her heart as she dropped the curtain and it swung in front of her, separating them again. She pushed it back, her eyes blazing. "What are you doing sneaking up on me?"

He couldn't even claim not to have been sneaking up on her because that's exactly what he'd been doing. "I didn't hear anything, so I thought Marina might be here."

Iris ran a hand through her dark curls absently and waved him back as she shook her head. "Why would Marina be here, of all places?"

Vaskel stepped into the back room, tipping his head to see the bookwyrms gliding high overhead as the skylights let in what gray winter light there was on offer. The chaos of the previous day was gone, but there was still an empty teacup and crumb-filled plate on the round table that centered the room.

He supposed there was no time like the present to tell Iris her friend was the hellkin's latest target. "Because I thought Cali might have brought her. We saw Cali with Marina in the castle this morning."

The apothecary whirled around, her long colorful skirt catching air and swirling at her ankles. "Why would Cali be at the castle? And why would she have anything to do with Marina?"

"Your guess is as good as ours how it all happened, but from what I could get from a drunk Thrain, Marina figured out that he had never run on a crew before but Cali had."

Iris's half-moon glasses slid so far down her nose Vaskel was sure they'd slip right off. "Does she know Cali crewed with you?"

He gave a clipped nod. "Thrain told her."

"Festering dragon dung," Iris muttered as she picked up the empty teacup, took a sip, and frowned when there was nothing to swallow. "That doesn't explain why Cali would consort with someone like Marina."

"Lira and I thought you could shed some light on that." Vaskel shifted from one foot to the other. "You've spent more time with her lately than either of us."

Iris nodded, studying him for a beat. "We do like to talk about the latest books I give her to read." She flicked a hand toward the cushy chairs in the corner. "She's spent many an hour reading here while I work."

"Do you think she's lonely? Do you think she might be vulnerable to the charms of a very cunning hellkin?"

Iris leveled her gaze at him over her glasses. "I think anyone could find themselves vulnerable to a very manipulative and very beautiful hellkin."

Ouch. Vaskel dropped his gaze, his face once again flashing unwanted heat.

Iris let out a heavy breath and closed the distance between them, resting a hand gently on his cursed arm. "I only mean that even the strongest can be swayed, especially when they are good at heart."

Vaskel raised his head and met her gaze and her smile. "I'd like to think that Cali is wiser and savvier than I was."

Iris shrugged. "If Marina is as good as you say she is, I'm sure

Cali believes she's just making a new friend. Maybe she's even convinced she's helping an old friend of yours. After all, Marina told Thrain that you two were friends from childhood."

Vaskel wanted to believe Iris. "But I saw the way Cali looked at Marina. She looked enchanted."

Iris's smile warmed, and her voice softened. "That's the problem with hellkins. They're very charming and very easy to fall for."

Vaskel's breath got stuck in his throat and his voice crackled when he could finally speak. "Iris, I—"

Before he could tell her that his attempts to charm her had been with only the best intentions and genuine affection, she spun again, disappearing into the even smaller back room where she kept her hot plate and boiled water for tea. "Enough of that. You probably need to find Cali and talk to her. We won't know if she's truly fallen under the hellkin's spell until then. But first, we need to talk about the potion I'm brewing."

Vaskel cleared his throat, adjusting to Iris's sudden shift in subject. "Sass should have popped by with the hairs she stole from Marina's room at the castle."

"She did, she did." Iris reemerged, making a beeline for him and reaching up a hand, as if to caress the side of his face.

Without thinking about it, Vaskel closed his eyes and leaned into the touch, forgetting everything he'd told himself about keeping his feelings hidden so he could keep Iris safe from Marina. Then her fingers tangled in his hair and tugged hard.

"Ouch!" He jerked away as Iris yanked a few hairs from his head, winking at him as she backed toward the attached room again.

She winked at him. "But we forgot yours, love."

Vaskel rubbed his head where he was now short some hair. At least the pain in his head was distracting him from the embarrassment of thinking Iris was caressing his face. He needed to get out of there before he completely humiliated himself.

"So the potion is nearly finished, then?"

Iris wiped her hands on each other as she joined him again. "Once all the hairs simmer a bit longer, it should be ready to use."

"Lira is working on the cookies we're going to use as the potion delivery device," Vaskel said. "If she perfects the recipe and you finish the potion, we should have a way to break the soul bind by tonight."

"Just in time," Iris reminded him. "Do you think Marina will come to the tavern to find you?"

"If she doesn't, I'll go find her." Determination surged through him anew. "Besides, I need to find out how far Marina has her claws into Cali."

Iris folded her arms over her chest. "I think it's about time we returned to having only one hellkin in Wayside."

Vaskel managed a teasing grin. "I hope that hellkin is me."

"It is." The tenderness in the apothecary's voice made the room go sideways for Vaskel, and he had to fight the urge to throw caution out the window and gather the woman into his arms. But before he could, she gave him a pat on the arm that was clearly a dismissal. "I'll bring the potion to the tavern when it's done. You find Cali."

He nodded, walking mutely through the curtain and the dimly lit shop. He barely noticed the bell announcing his departure, and only when the icy air hit him did he snap out of his daze of wishfulness.

Vaskel turned to walk back to the tavern, but stopped so quickly he nearly stumbled over his own feet.

"Impossible," he whispered to himself, staring at the now-empty spot on the road leading to the castle. A few blinks ago, he'd been sure he'd seen Erindil dressed like a rogue.

Thirty-Seven

THERE WAS no way the figure he'd spotted in the distance was Erindil, Vaskel told himself as he bustled through the village, the hood of his cloak flipped over his head so he could avoid being pulled into conversations. He tossed quick waves to both Fenni and Pip, giving silent thanks that Tin hadn't spotted him. He wasn't sure if his excuses would matter to the enthusiastic haberdasher.

Vaskel tried to focus on finding Cali, but his mind continued to circle back to the strange elf sighting. Why would Erindil be wearing oddly subdued clothes? He'd never seen Lira's uncle dressed in anything but ornate robes. The thought of Erindil in snug pants and a long tunic was so absurd he almost laughed out loud.

No, his mind had been playing tricks on him. Maybe it was the effects of the marks crawling up his arms. Maybe it was his worry over Cali.

Cali. Iris had tasked him with finding Cali and talking to her, which was what he was going to do, oddly dressed elf or not.

Swinging his head from side to side, he caught no glimpse of the pantheri. Not that he suspected he would. If she wasn't at the tavern or the apothecary's, then she must be with Marina. Neither of them spent much free time in their small rooms at the inn, and his hellkin instincts told him he'd find his friend at the castle.

A few flakes of snow sifted lazily through the air as he crossed the bridge, the rhythmic clang of the blacksmith's hammer calming his nerves as he thought about encountering Marina or her hellkin crew. It didn't matter how much he dreaded seeing Marina. He would do it for Cali.

He curled his hands into tight balls by his side as he strode toward the castle, the trees bowing snow-laden branches toward him and darkening the road.

Vaskel clocked a pair of guards at two corner towers, their presence reassuring him. At least Marina and her crew hadn't taken over the castle. At least there were still guards.

He walked beneath the portcullis, exhaling when he spotted Val. The blonde was in her full uniform with quilted chest armor and a sword hitched to her belt.

"I've got this," Val called out to the other guard in the courtyard, although Vaskel didn't see the other man—who looked like he also might be part goblin—make a move to help.

"I thought I might see you," Val said when she was close enough to Vaskel that no one could overhear them. "I thought you might come looking for Cali."

"Do you know where she is?"

Val snuck a glance over one shoulder and dropped her voice to a whisper. "Last I heard, she and Marina were dining in the great hall."

Vaskel swore to himself. He couldn't let Marina see him trying to talk to Cali. That would only make her sink her claws in deeper.

"But Marina usually attends the laird in the afternoon," Val continued. "There's a good chance you can grab Cali then."

"I doubt I'll be doing any grabbing." Vaskel let out a dark, mirthless laugh. "Cali isn't some damsel in distress I can throw over my shoulder."

Val's brows popped high. "Not unless you want an arrow in your back."

"All I need is a few minutes to talk to her, but it has to be alone."

Val nodded, her expression serious. "I can stand guard and make sure Marina doesn't surprise you. Be warned, though. Marina has managed to sweet-talk the rest of the guards. They're convinced she's going to heal the laird and return this castle to its glory days. They won't hear a word against her. Neither will the laird's advisors. So, if we get caught…"

"We won't," he promised.

Val squared her shoulders. "Come with me." Her voice boomed across the courtyard, making Vaskel jump, and she strode toward an arched doorway, glancing back at him. "Don't make me wait."

Vaskel recognized her loud voice as a show she was putting on for the other guards, although none of them seemed to care or notice. Still, Vaskel followed her.

The air in the dimly lit corridors was dank, but soon Vaskel's nose twitched from the scent of something rich and savory. They were approaching the kitchen or the banquet hall.

When they reached a pair of heavy wooden doors, Val held up a fist. She creaked one door open a crack, peeking inside and then breathing a sigh. "The hellkin's gone. It looks like Cali is finishing her meal alone." She opened the door fully, locking eyes with him as he passed. "Good luck."

Vaskel stepped into the large room, realizing that he was entering from the back. Long tables stretched the length of the otherwise empty hall, and every clink of Cali's silverware echoed off the stone walls and vaulted ceiling. He took long steps until he was dropping into the chair beside her at the long table on the dais.

The pantheri twitched, her gold eyes flaring as she turned to him. "What are you doing here?"

"I came to talk to you." Vaskel narrowed his gaze at her. "What are you doing here?"

"Helping," Cali said, turning back to her plate. "The traveling healer needed my help."

"Marina," Vaskel said, fighting to keep the disdain from his voice.

Cali's whiskers quivered. "She said she knew you."

Vaskel had already heard from Thrain that Marina was passing them off as childhood friends, but his past wasn't why he'd come.

"Cal, Marina isn't who she says she is."

The archer smiled. "She also said you'd say that."

Vaskel clenched his teeth to keep from shaking his friend and shouting that Marina was twisting the truth. "Cal—"

"It's nice to be needed again," Cali said before he could finish. "I didn't know how much I missed it. Don't get me wrong, it's been great reuniting the crew in Wayside, but a part of me misses the quests, the purpose, the chance to use my skills. You and Lira have the tavern, and even Rog has Rosie have their brandy cart. I have..."

Vaskel swallowed hard as her words drifted off. "You're a little lost is all. It happens to all of us once we stop crewing. You'll find something great to do."

The pantheri twisted her head to meet his gaze. "What if I already have? What if joining a new crew is my something great?"

Vaskel bit back all the horrible truths he wanted to tell her about Marina. "What about our crew? You said yourself that we're the family we chose. That doesn't come along every day, Cal."

"True, but does that mean I give up on it?"

Vaskel had felt lost before. Hells and cinders, he'd felt just like Cali had before he'd found their crew. He understood loneliness. He understood her desire to have a purpose.

She leaned close to him. "Don't you miss the adventure, Vask? Don't you miss the joy of completing a quest?"

He thought about the rush he used to feel after they'd collected their bounty. It had been great, but it had been fleeting. It also hadn't been the kind of happiness that settled into your bones.

"If you ask me, the greatest parts of life are what happens between all the quests and adventures," he said. "Sitting around the fire after a mission and laughing about our narrow escape. Catching a perfect sunset on the trek to collect our gold. Licking sugar off your fingers from Pip's lemon sweet rolls—if you were lucky enough to get one after Sass got to them. We have to enjoy the little things in life because, in the end, those are the things that matter."

A reluctant smile teased Cali's mouth. "I will miss Pip's sweet rolls."

Vaskel's heart lurched. "You aren't serious about leaving, are you, Cali? I can help you find something that makes you feel alive again. We all can."

Cali opened her mouth and then closed it again. "I'm sorry, Vask. Adventure, bounties, quests? It's too tempting to pass up."

Of course it was. Marina knew exactly how to tempt each of her marks.

Before he could argue for Cali to stay, a whistle pierced the air. They hadn't discussed a signal, but Vaskel knew this was Val's way of telling him he needed to leave.

Vaskel squeezed one hand on Cali's gray-striped arm. "You're my family, Cali. I don't want to lose you." Then he got up and ran toward the door, slipping through it just as he heard Marina's voice fill the hall.

He paused, glancing back through the crack in the door as it slid shut. Marina was next to Cali, one hand resting on the archer's furry arm as she gazed at her with an intoxicating intensity that Vaskel knew all too well.

Val wasn't waiting in the hall anymore, which Vaskel was glad for. He wouldn't have wanted her to see the tear that slid down his face as he hurried away.

Thirty-Eight

VASKEL'S STEPS back to Wayside and the Tusk & Tail were leaden, his boots trodding on the packed snow, and before he knew it, he was staring in front of the tavern. He held open the front door for a farmer with a wispy mustache who was leaving with a half-eaten scone in one hand. The familiar scents of sugar and spice made the hellkin's shoulders uncoil as he walked inside.

Lira was right that baking was a special kind of magic. Even before a single sip of chai or a bite of a buttery, crumbly scone, he felt more at ease.

Sass worked her way around the wooden tables, a tray of scones held high over her head. Folks were sipping chai from ceramic mugs, low conversation humming between them and melding with the crackle of the fire.

The afternoon scone service was always a more mellow experience than nighttime at the tavern, when ale flowed as freely as the raucous tales.

Lira stepped from the kitchen with a tray of mugs, sliding it onto the top of the long bar. Her gaze fell on Vaskel, and her brows rose in an unspoken question.

He continued past his usual post behind the bar, following her back into the kitchen where there was less chance of them being overheard. The doors swung shut behind him, but Lira waited until he scraped the stool across the floor to the worktable and sat down.

"So?" she asked him as both Crumpet and Bramble perched on their hind legs as if just as eager to hear his answer. "What did Iris have to say about Cali?"

He'd been so distracted by seeing Cali that he'd almost forgotten visiting Iris for her take on the situation.

"I saw Cali." He schooled his tail so it wouldn't flick behind him and reveal his inner turmoil. "Iris suggested I talk to her, which was good advice, so I tracked her down at the castle."

Lira braced her hands on the wooden table and leaned forward. "And?"

"I talked to her." He considered how much to tell Lira, how much more to put on her, but he decided on the truth—all of it. "She's felt lost here since we all have something to do and she doesn't. She misses the purpose of quests. I think she misses the camaraderie more, and she thinks she'll get that again with Marina."

Lira gnawed at her bottom lip, finally throwing a dishtowel on the table and making the flutterstoat and raccoon flinch. "This is my fault. I should have been paying more attention to

Cal. This is my hometown. I should have made sure she was happy here."

Vaskel shook his head so hard his long hair swished around his neck. "You couldn't have known. Neither could I. I thought she was happy reading and taking it easy. I thought she was enjoying a break after so many years adventuring."

Lira ran a hand through her hair, leaving a streak of flour in it. "We have to intervene and tell her we can fix this—together, like we always have. We have to get Cali away from that hellkin's clutches."

Vaskel eyed the pot of bubbling chai, his stomach snarling at him. "I told her all that. We can't exactly kidnap her."

"Says who?" Lira started pacing a small circle behind the table, and both Crumpet and Bramble backed away with wide eyes. "It's not kidnapping if it's for a noble reason."

"Not sure that's the way it works," Vaskel said in a low voice that Lira didn't hear.

"Maybe we can lure her with Pip's sweet rolls," Lira muttered. "She loves those."

Vaskel groaned as he imagined Lira setting up a trap with sweet rolls tied to a string. "For the moment, Cali is safe, especially since Marina believes she's got her fooled."

"Which she does," Lira grumbled but stopped pacing.

"For now, but Cal is smart. Marina can't keep up the ruse forever. We should focus on thwarting Marina and her hellkin crew. Then we can get Cali without putting her at risk."

Lira followed Vaskel's gaze as it drifted to the chai again. She reached for a mug, pouring the amber liquid until it nearly reached the rim. She slid him the mug, then grabbed an overly browned scone from an otherwise empty baking pan—one no doubt deemed too imperfect to serve—and tossed it to him.

Vaskel snatched it from the air with his free hand, grinning that Lira hadn't forgotten his quick reflexes—or lost her aim. He sipped the chai and bit into the scone, the cinnamon in both warming him from the inside as he swallowed.

"That's the plan?" Lira asked, tapping her toe on the floor in rapid fire.

Crumpet folded his tiny, furry arms and mimicked the movement with his own white foot, narrowing his ink-drop eyes as if just as frustrated as his mistress.

Vaskel fought the urge to laugh and almost choked as he swallowed a mouthful of scone. He gulped the chai and wiped the grin from his face. He didn't want to incur Lira's or Crumpet's wrath.

"I suggest we work even harder on the cookies that will break the soul bind. Once we break Marina's power over me, she won't have a reason to stay in Wayside, especially if we show her how clearly she isn't welcome."

Lira's downturned mouth twitched up. "Should I assemble the villagers? Our little armed mob made an impression on the dwarf hunting party that tried to come for Sass."

Armed might have been overstating it a bit since some of the villagers' weapons had been cheese knives and fabric shears. He shook his head. "I don't want to put anyone else at risk. Not unless our hand is forced."

"If Marina tries to do anything to you or Cali, consider my hand forced," Lira said, "but I can keep working on the potion cookies if you're sure that's the best plan."

Vaskel wasn't sure of anything anymore, but he knew his time was running out. "For now. Iris promised to bring the potion here as soon as it was ready."

Vaskel took another sip of chai, hoping the spicy tea would drown all his worries.

Thirty-Nine

THE TUSK & Tail thrummed with life, laughter rolling through the great room in waves that reached the smoke-darkened rafters.

Vaskel pulled ales absently, sliding tankards down the bar to waiting hands while keeping up a stream of banter with the regulars. The familiar rhythm of greeting, pouring, and serving kept his hands busy and his mind blessedly occupied. No time to think about Marina or soul binds or even Cali's notable absence.

In their usual armchairs by the hearth, Korl and Val had

claimed their evening spots early. Val's knitting needles clicked steadily as she worked on what appeared to be the world's longest scarf, the white wool pooling to the floor like a yarn waterfall. Korl nursed the same tankard of ale he'd had since the early afternoon, his gaze on the fire with an occasional glance toward the kitchen doors.

At one of the long tables, Thrain and Rog had begun their nightly competition of tall tales, and it was good to see that the dwarf had bounced back from his heartbreak.

"—and that's when the troll sneezed, sending me flying straight through the window of the temple." Rog slammed a hand onto the table and made a pewter plate jump.

"A troll sneeze?" Thrain scoffed. "That's nothing. I once arm-wrestled an ice giant for the right to cross a bridge in the Ice Lands."

"Won, did ya?" the gnome asked, stroking his beard with one hand.

Thrain leaned forward. "Nah. Had to go the long way. That's why it took me so long to reach Wayside."

Rog barked a laugh, and they both rocked back on the benches, slapping their knees and then each other's backs.

Lira emerged from the kitchen, her cheeks pink from the oven's heat, wisps of hair escaping from her braid. She looked tired but content, the way she always did after a successful evening of feeding the masses. Although this time the evening rush was far from over.

"Everything okay?" Vaskel asked as he moved to the end of the bar nearest the kitchen. There was more meaning than usual in his question, and Lira met his gaze with a knowing look of her own.

"The recipe is perfected. The cookies are rich and flavorful with enough of a brandy punch to mask anything."

He tilted his head. "No samples?"

Sass walked up to them, slapping her empty tray on the bar top and heaving a sigh. Sweat beaded her brow, as much from the fire as from her work serving food. "Are we talking about meat pies? If so, I just passed out the last of them."

Lira's gaze held the dwarf's as she gave her a wry smile. "Vaskel asked if there were any samples of the dark chocolate brandy cookies."

Dark splotches appeared on Sass's brown cheeks—the dwarven version of a blush. "Aye, well, someone had to taste test them."

"And finish them," Lira added.

Sass's mouth dropped, her spluttering defense lost as Vaskel and Lira burst into laughter. Sass huffed with mock offense before flouncing back to the floor. She made her way to Val's chair, perching on the overstuffed arm and leaning close to say something that made the guardswoman's stern face soften into a smile.

"It's a good feeling when people you love find their people, isn't it?" Lira said softly, watching the pair with affection.

"It is," Vaskel agreed, "but I suppose that isn't totally accurate. True love isn't found, it's built."

Lira had returned to Wayside and found Korl, discovering her one and only in the last place she'd expected, but it had been patience and kindness that had built their foundation. Sass had been on the run from an arranged marriage, only to stumble into Wayside and straight into Val's steady, patient heart, but the pair had put in lots of time learning how to be with each other.

Lira smiled softly at him. "Look who's so wise in the ways of love."

Vaskel shrugged. Maybe the village was charmed, some kind of benevolent magic that drew lonely souls together and gave them what they needed to build love.

Then he thought about his own luck—soul-bound to a vindictive hellkin, marks spreading across his skin like poison, pushing away the one person his heart desired. Maybe Wayside's charm only worked for those who were worthy, not for hellkins with dodgy pasts and too many regrets.

Lira's voice snapped him from the torment of his thoughts, but he hadn't heard what she'd said. "Pardon?"

Lira stepped closer to him, touching his arm. "I said that all we need now is for Iris to come and bring me the final ingredient."

Even though they were standing close enough for their conversation to be private and even though the din of the tavern was enough to drown out their words, Lira didn't dare mention the potion. Vaskel appreciated that she still operated as if they were in the midst of a dangerous quest. In a way, they were, and this one held his own fate in the balance.

"She'll come," Vaskel said with complete certainty. Like all his friends in his adopted home, he trusted Iris with his life.

"I'm not worried about Iris coming through for us. I'm worried about Cali."

Vaskel held the same concern, but he also held tight to the belief that their former crew mate was clever and cunning in her own right. She was a pantheri, after all, with feline reflexes and the instincts of a predator. If anyone could snap out of Marina's grasp, it was Cali.

Before he could remind Lira of all the reasons they should have faith in the archer, the tavern door swung open. Holding his breath, Vaskel glanced toward the light spilling out into the steady snowfall, releasing a grateful breath that it was the apothecary outlined in the doorway and not the hellkin.

Iris stepped inside, throwing back her cloak's hood and shaking off snowflakes that instantly melted onto the floor. Her hair was a tangle of dark curls and her cheeks were pink from the cold. Her gaze swept the great room, taking only an instant to find him behind the bar. Her eyes crinkled into a smile, but Vaskel winced at the weariness etched into her face.

She didn't waste any time winding her way through the crowd to reach Vaskel and Lira, although she kept her hands tucked safely beneath her forest green cloak until she reached them.

"Is it ready?" Lira asked in a low voice.

Iris nodded, parting the front of her cloak enough to reveal a small, bulbous bottle filled with a murky brown liquid.

Lira made a face but took it, keeping her hand low as she slipped it beneath her apron.

"How long will it take to make them?" the apothecary asked, hiding her now-empty hands under her cloak again.

"Not long," Lira said, already backing away. "A few minutes to mix up the batter and no more than ten to bake them. The oven is already hot."

Iris managed a smile and a nod as Lira ducked into the kitchen, leaving the half doors swinging in her wake.

Once she was gone, Vaskel eyed Iris. "Why did you ask that? It wasn't idle curiosity."

The woman's smile became sad. "You know me a bit too well. I wanted to know because we might have less time than we thought."

Fear slid cool talons around Vaskel's heart. "Why do you say that?"

Iris's gaze flitted to the kitchen doors then back to him. "Because I saw Cali. She stopped by the shop."

He snatched a breath. "You saw her too?"

"She came by to return the books she'd borrowed from me, Vask. All of them."

The talons pierced his heart. Cali would only do that if she were leaving, which meant he might have been wrong about the archer and her ability to resist Marina.

Forty

LIRA STOOD BACK from the metal baking sheet after pouring hot glaze over the four large cookies. "There they are."

Vaskel, Sass, and Iris stood on the other side of the wooden work table, eyeing the knobby, glossy cookies. Lira had packed them with dark chocolate, tart cherries, and a potion that would hopefully break a soul bind, before smothering them in a chocolate glaze.

Both Crumpet and Bramble were sitting on the sill of the open window, as if prepared to depart hastily if anything went wrong.

The flutterstoat narrowed his eyes at the cookies, wagging a finger at his raccoon friend, presumably warning him not to steal bites of these baked treats.

Sass shoved up the sleeves of her puffy white blouse. "What now? Do we taste them?"

Lira arched a brow at the dwarf. "You didn't get enough earlier?"

"You asked for a taste tester," Sass grumbled. "I was trying to help."

Iris tapped a finger on her chin. "I don't suppose it would harm someone who doesn't have a soul bind to ingest the potion, but I honestly don't know enough about it to say for sure."

"Isn't this your uncle's potion?" Sass asked. "Shouldn't we ask him?"

Iris blew out a breath. "That's a fine idea. Erindil didn't mention the potential dangers of the potion or even how much should be taken."

Sass spun on her heel and headed for the swinging doors. "On it."

Lira frowned. "That would have been helpful to know before I put the potion in the batter." She took a flat spatula and lifted one of the four cookies from the tray. "I used all the potion in the bottle and didn't make a large batch."

Vaskel picked up the cookie that Lira had placed on an earthenware plate. He raised it to his nose and sniffed it. It didn't smell foul. The only aromas he could detect were the richness of the chocolate and the kick of the apple brandy. "They smell delicious."

Lira nibbled the corner of her lower lip. "I hope that doesn't mean they're too weak. We can't count on Marina eating more than one of these."

"I think it's a good sign," Iris said. "If they had enough potion in them so you could smell it, I doubt we could get her to eat more than one."

Suddenly, Vaskel was struck by something he hadn't bothered

to consider before. He braced his hands on the table as he dropped his head between his arms and groaned. "How are we going to get her to eat any?"

"What?" Lira asked.

Vaskel looked up, meeting Lira's confused gaze. "I mean, how do we give Marina cookies without it seeming suspicious? I can't walk up to her and offer her one. She'd see through me in a second."

"Son of a wand waxer," Lira cursed.

A strangled laugh escaped Iris. "I guess I was so focused on brewing the potion that I didn't think that even if we snuck it into something more palatable, we still had to find a way for her to want to ingest it."

"I'm not opposed to force-feeding the hellkin a cookie," Lira said, sliding the rest of the treats from the pan to the plate.

"It's too late to ask Pip to lure her into his shop and offer her a free cookie, and so far today, she hasn't shown her face inside the tavern." Vaskel muttered some choice hellkin curses under his breath. "And she probably won't if she's preparing to leave."

He didn't say the part that they were all thinking. She was preparing to leave and take Cali and him with her, since his three days were nearly gone.

"We still have options," Lira said, her voice more shrill than usual. "We've faced more dire situations than this, Vask. We just have to think."

Vaskel didn't remind her that when they'd faced those dire situations, they had the strength of their entire crew. They'd had Malek's talents and Pirrin's blade, Cali's stealth and Rog's bravery. Now, it was just down to them.

The doors swung open again, and Erindil swept into the kitchen with the gravitas of someone being announced at court.

"Greetings, my friends. This delightful dwarf tells me you require my assistance."

"Sass," the dwarf in question said as she rolled her eyes.

"Yes, yes." Erindil bestowed a glorious smile on her. "Dear little Sass."

Sass bristled, but before she could show Erindil her displeasure at being called little, Lira cleared her throat.

"We added the potion to the cookie batter, but now we don't know if it will be enough to do the job."

"Ah, yes." Erindil bent over to examine the cookies, squinting one eye. "How much potion went into the batter?"

Lira held up the empty glass bottle. "This much."

Erindil nodded thoughtfully. "I see. Very good, very good." Then he counted the cookies on the plate. "From what I can remember, it doesn't take a lot of potion to break the bind." He held up a slender finger. "It does, however, require both those bound to consume it at the same time."

Vaskel bit back another groan. So they had to contrive a reason for Marina to eat at least one cookie while he was also eating one. All without arousing the suspicions of a naturally suspicious hellkin.

Iris put a hand on his back. "Don't worry. We'll come up with a way to trick Marina into eating one."

Sass looked from Iris to Vaskel and shook her head. "Is that why you look like you just stepped in dragon dung? Well, it's simple isn't it?"

Lira stared at her friend. "Is it?"

"Aye." Sass jerked her head toward the great room. "We get Thrain to take them to her. He can pretend he's trying to win her back. He can even say that Pip made them. No offense, Lira, but everyone knows the halfling is a baking genius."

"If your plan works," Lira said, "no offense taken."

Erindil scrunched his lips to one side. "And is Thrain a good liar?"

Sass grinned. "He's never met a tall tale he couldn't make taller."

Forty-One

"AYE." Thrain dragged a hand down his beard before his fingers snagged on a tangle and he had to jerk them out. "I could persuade Marina to eat some cookies."

He sat at one of the long tavern tables, the plate of dark potion-filled cookies in front of him and Vaskel, Lira, Sass, Iris, and Erindil standing across the table from him. Korl and Val sat in their massive upholstered chairs by the spluttering fire, but the rest of the patrons were gone, although the tables still held the occasional emptied tankard or pewter plate littered with scraps of pastry crust.

Sass had just waved off the last customer, but hadn't finished cleaning the place. They'd all agreed it was more important to get Thrain on board with their plan than it was to polish all the glasses behind the bar and sweep the floors.

"I can make quick work of that while Thrain's off making cow eyes at the hellkin," Sass had said when they'd decided to approach Thrain, although not within earshot of the dwarf in question.

Lira braced her hands on the table and leaned forward. "You're sure you can convince her it's an attempt to win her back, so she won't be suspicious?"

Thrain shifted on the wooden bench. "If I didn't know what I do now, I might try to win her back. I might not have thought of cookies, though."

Sass jutted one hip out as she stared at her friend. "You're going to have to convince her you would. Remember, Pip made these, and they're a special recipe he created just for you to give her. That should sweeten the pot."

Lira frowned at this as Crumpet chittered indignantly on her shoulder. "Do you really think they'd be less appealing if she thought I baked them."

Iris patted the woman's arm. "You're too close to Vaskel. If she knows you crewed together, she might suspect you of having ulterior motives. No one would suspect Pip of doing anything covert."

Vaskel grunted his agreement. "She's met and charmed Pip. She's also tasted his baking. I can't imagine her not being tempted by the idea of treats created specially for her by him."

"Fine." Lira sniffed, with the fultterstoat mimicking the action with a haughty jerk of his tiny chin. "But if this works, I want credit for making the cookies that broke a soul bind."

"We can put a sign outside the tavern if you want," Sass told her with a grin. "Although I doubt that will have folks beating down our doors."

Lira shot her a look but seemed mollified. Crumpet seemed less so.

"When do I need to take her the cookies?" Thrain asked.

"Tonight," Vaskel said before anyone else could speak. "It has to be tonight."

He didn't explain that he was running out of time before Marina came to claim him or that Cali was planning to leave with the hellkin. He didn't need to. Thrain was enough of a loyal friend that he didn't require explanations.

The dwarf nodded and then shrugged. "As good a time as any, I suppose."

He reached for the plate, but Sass shooed his hands away.

"You aren't going to take them like that." She produced a slightly crumpled paper bag from the pocket of her full skirt. "This is one of Pip's bakery bags. It'll be more convincing."

"Good thinking," Iris said.

Lira eyed her, lips twitching. "You happened to have a bakery bag on you?"

Sass straightened as if affronted. "You never know when you might need a bag."

"Mm-hmm." Lira's lips curled into a wry smile. "It wouldn't have anything to do with the last sweet roll that went missing a few days ago, would it?"

"Don't know what you're going on about." Sass unfurled the bag and began sliding the cookies into it.

Vaskel stopped her before she added the last cookie to the bag. "I need one to eat at the same time Marina's ingesting hers."

Thrain's forehead bunched. "How's this going to work then? I find Marina, pretend I'm desperate to win her back and offer her a gift, and then what?" He locked eyes with Vaskel. "How are you going to know when she's eating the cookie?"

"I'll have to go with you," Vaskel said, "but I'll stay far enough away that I'm not spotted."

"What if she's in the castle?" Thrain asked. "There aren't a lot of places to hide in those corridors, and if she invites me into her room, you won't have any way of knowing what's going on."

Iris exhaled heavily. "He's right. There are too many variables we can't control."

"We don't need to control all of them." Erindil spoke for the first time since they'd approached Thrain. "We only need to figure out a way to get eyes on Marina."

Lira turned to her uncle. "I don't know everything about elvish powers, but I didn't think you could make yourself invisible or see through walls."

He chuckled. "I can't, my dear, although wouldn't that be delightful fun?"

Vaskel fought the urge to roll his eyes at the elf who seemed to move through life as if nothing was ever worth fretting over. Perhaps if he lived thousands of years, he might feel the same way. As it was, he only lived a few hundred, and he didn't want to spend the last half of his life bound to Marina.

"How do you suggest we get eyes on Marina then?" Vaskel asked.

Erindil put a hand to his face, drumming his long fingers slowly on his jawline. Then he rested his gaze on Lira, a grin spreading across his face. "Why didn't I think of it before?"

"What?" Vaskel and Lira said at the same time.

Erindil pointed a regal finger at Lira. "Isn't it obvious?"

Vaskel stared at his friend, wondering what he was missing. As far as he knew, the half-elf woman had fewer powers than her uncle, and even those were hardly controllable.

"Me?" Lira blinked rapidly.

Erindil laughed, draping his hand on his niece's arm. "Not you, dear, although I can see why you might think that." He raised his finger to point directly at Crumpet. "Him."

Everyone in the great room swiveled their eyes to the white, winged stoat with black markings around his eyes that gave him the unmistakable look of a bandit.

"You want me to take the wee beastie with me?" Thrain asked, looking baffled by the suggestion.

"No." Erindil shook his head. "I don't think that would be very subtle. Our little friend here is quite distinctive."

Sass tilted her head. "And clearly enchanted, which is why we keep him out of sight of most folks."

"But he can fly, can't he?" Erindil reached up and scruffed the little creature's head. "Which means he could reach windows."

"Which could be the same as being able to see through walls," Lira said, a look of understanding passing over her face.

Erindil bobbed his head up and down. "Vaskel can take our winged friend with him, and if Thrain goes into a room he can't follow, the little fellow could fly to the window and signal Vaskel when to eat the potion cookie."

"This seems only slightly less risky," Iris said. "What if there's no window?"

"It might be the best we can do," Lira told her. "That is, if Crumpet is willing."

The flutterstoat cocked his head to one side, as if considering, then let loose a stream of chatter and flew from Lira's shoulder to Vaskel's.

Vaskel reached up and extended a finger for Crumpet to shake. "I think that's a yes."

Thrain pushed away from the table and stood. "We'd better get going then."

Sass handed him the bag of cookies when he'd walked around the table. "Don't mess this up."

His belly shook with a rough laugh. "Nothing like a pep talk from Sass."

"Wait, it's just the two of you?" Iris asked, ignoring Crumpet's chattering protest at not being counted. "Shouldn't you have backup?"

"I'm happy to go with them," Erindil said. "I'm quite good at staying out of sight."

Vaskel eyed the elf's velvet robes that flared out behind him. Unobtrusive wasn't a word he'd associated with the Lira's uncle, but he would also never turn down help from an elf.

Korl stood from his overstuffed chair. "I can come too."

"Count me in," Val said, as she dumped her knitting on the floor.

Erindil put a hand on the orc's sizable arm. "I don't think you've ever stayed out of sight, dear boy. But perhaps you and Val could remain outside the castle in case the hellkin tries to run."

Vaskel gave the assembled team a curt nod. "Shall we?"

He made a move toward the door but Iris stepped in front of him. "I hope this will work, but in case it...I mean, if you can't break the bind...oh, hells and cinders." She reached up, grabbed his lapels, and yanked his mouth to hers.

Vaskel's body reacted instantly, his lips softening and heat pulsing through his veins and pounding in his ears.

Then Iris released him and stepped back, her cheeks flaming. "For luck."

He attempted to say something, but words failed him. Finally Sass thumped him hard on the back. "I also wish you luck, Vask, but not *that* much."

<h1 style="text-align:center">Forty-Two</h1>

VASKEL WALKED WOODENLY from the tavern, Crumpet riding on his shoulder. Beside him, Thrain cleared his throat and swung his arms as he took long steps to keep pace with the hellkin and elf.

"No one kissed me for good luck," the dwarf groused as they headed down the snow-trodden road toward the bridge.

"Nor me," Erindil said, his hands folded neatly in front of him as he walked, "although my future doesn't hang in the balance."

"Sass kissed me," Val called from where she and Korl were bringing up the rear of the party.

Thrain stole a look at Vaskel. "You have more to lose than the rest of us. You think that's why she kissed you?"

Vaskel wanted to say that he didn't know why Iris had kissed him, but that would have been a lie. She'd kissed him for the very reason he'd been making excuses to visit her shop, although he sorely wished that he'd known she felt the same before this moment.

"The apothecary clearly has feelings for our charming hellkin friend." Erindil tipped his head to Vaskel. "Not that anyone could blame her. You're a handsome chap, if you don't mind horns."

"Thanks," Vaskel muttered, reasonably sure that had been a compliment.

"You and Iris, eh?" Thrain nodded slowly. "You could have mentioned something, you know."

"There was nothing to mention." Vaskel's lips still buzzed from the kiss, and he wrestled the urge to press his fingers to his mouth.

"That kiss begged to differ," Val said.

Thrain's laugh was a rumble that shook his chest. "Aye, it did."

Crumpet chittered softly, as if agreeing with the guard and the dwarf.

Vaskel's mind whirled as thoughts of Iris flooded his head—her fierce expression as she'd pulled him to her, the dazed look in her eyes when she'd released him, and the softness of her mouth against his. For a moment, he forgot where they were going entirely.

"As much as I delight in discussing romance," Erindil said, "we should focus on the task at hand, don't you think?"

Vaskel gave his head a brief shake, as if to dislodge thoughts of Iris. "We should. Marina isn't someone to underestimate. She's clever and usually one step ahead of everyone else."

"Except for us." Thrain jerked a thumb toward his chest. "This time we've got the advantage."

Vaskel wasn't sure if that was true. They had some things in their favor, but Marina was no easy mark.

As they approached the bridge, he looked down the main village thoroughfare, but it was deserted. The shops were dark, and the market stalls shuttered and empty. Only a distant neigh from the stables and an even more faraway hoot of an owl broke the winter night's hush.

"You said she's staying at the castle," the elf asked, his gaze going to the stone edifice peeking over the treetops.

Vaskel made a gruff sound in his throat. "Pretending to be a healer." He remembered spotting the elf heading to the castle. "You've been there recently, haven't you?"

"Me?" Erindil shook his head. "At the castle? My dear boy, I've been at the encampment all day. You must be mistaken." He frowned. "But you're not the first person to think they've seen me somewhere I haven't been. That dear halfling baker was certain he'd sold me a bag of sweet rolls when I hadn't even set foot in the village that day."

"Is it possible you have a twin?" Vaskel asked.

The elf looked scandalized by this suggestion. "Absolutely not. There is no one exactly like me."

"I'll agree with that," Thrain said, shooting Erindil a side-eye glance.

"You sure you don't want us to smooth the way with the castle guards?" Val called up as they crossed the ice-slicked bridge.

"Too much fuss," Thrain answered before Vaskel could. "The guards have seen me there before with Marina. They'll let me through, especially if I sell them my sad story of heartbreak."

Vaskel had to admire the way the dwarf had bounced back from his rejection. He'd seen lesser men fall into despair over the beautiful hellkin.

Once they were over the bridge, they took the path leading to the castle, with Val and Korl dropping farther and farther behind.

"We'll wait here," Korl said when they were within sight of the castle entrance.

"You need anything," Val added, straightening her quilted chest armor. "You call out."

Vaskel hesitated before continuing, locking eyes with Korl for a moment. "If I don't—"

"You will," the orc interrupted before he could finish. "You have to stand up with me at my wedding."

Vaskel's throat tightened, and he pressed his lips together, unable to speak.

Korl gave a sharp nod, as if it had been decided. "We'll see you when it's done."

Thrain rocked back on his heels, glancing between Korl and Vaskel and clearing his throat. Even Crumpet cooed softly on Vaskel's shoulder.

Only Erindil seemed unaffected, rubbing his hands when they continued on their journey and left Korl and Val behind. "I suppose we shouldn't all go inside the castle either, although I don't know how much help I can be if I don't know what's happening."

"I'll go inside alone," Thrain announced as the stone walls of the castle loomed larger. "That makes the most sense. If Marina is in her room, that's one floor up on the west wing."

Three doors down, if Vaskel remembered correctly from when he'd seen Sass emerge from it.

"Try to talk loud or give me some kind of sign," he told the dwarf. "Then Crumpet can fly up and find you easier."

Thrain grunted. "I can do that." A grin split his whiskers. "I might even manage a bit of wailing."

"Don't overdo it," Vaskel warned, even though his lips twitched. "Marina might see through fake heartbreak."

"Who's faking? That woman broke my heart clean in two."

Vaskel rested a hand on the dwarf's shoulders. "I want you to know how much I appreciate you doing this for me. I know it isn't easy, and I'm sorry you got sucked into it."

"You're not to blame for my foolishness, and you don't need to thank me. You'd do the same for me."

Vaskel squeezed Thrain's shoulder. He was right. He would risk himself for the dwarf or any of his friends in Wayside. He'd come to the village knowing only Lira and Cali, but since then he'd added so many to his chosen family. Some days it was hard to think back to times when he'd been alone and believed there was no place in the Known Lands he would ever think of as a true home.

"Very good," Erindil said, "but that leaves me without a way to lend aid if needed."

Thrain readjusted his grip on the paper bakery bag. "I didn't say you couldn't come in. I just said I should go in alone."

The elf's eyes widened. "I see. I can enter the castle grounds after you and for an entirely different purpose." He rapped a finger on his chin. "What that is, I'm not entirely sure, but I'll come up with something." His pensive expression dissolved into a smile. "It's been quite a while since I've stormed a castle, but this should be good fun."

Thrain's brows climbed higher. "Not sure if I'd call this storming the castle, but I'm glad to know you'll be near."

"Good luck all," Vaskel said with a last look and nod.

"Aye." Thrain wagged a stubby finger at the hellkin. "Save your kiss for Iris, though."

Vaskel shot him another look before backing away and peeling off before the guards at the castle gate spotted him. Crumpet shifted his stance on his shoulder, chittering gently as they left the path.

The brush was thick around the castle walls, more evidence that the place was slipping. He lifted his knees high, stepping through the tangle of frozen vines and trying to avoid the icy puddles of sludge pooling around the stone walls.

Tipping back his head, he peered up the towering stone bathed in moonlight. Sharp icicles hung from the top of the castle like bared teeth, and he muttered a prayer to the infernal gods to not be gored by a falling one.

When Vaskel had walked along the western wall to the window he estimated to be Marina's, he stopped. "That should be it. It's one of the few with a lantern lit inside. That's a good sign, right?"

Crumpet chattered an answer that he hoped was agreement.

"It shouldn't be long now," he said in a voice loud enough for the flutterstoat on his shoulder. "Then we can go back to the tavern and life can go back to normal."

But things couldn't go back to normal for him and Iris. Not after that kiss.

He released a visible breath. "I suppose I'll have to tell Iris how I feel."

Crumpet's chattering about this was more pointed, and unless the hellkin was imagining things, a bit judgmental.

"Yes, I suppose I should have told her sooner." He flicked a gaze toward the flutterstoat without turning his head. "But I was afraid of ruining our friendship."

Crumpet blew a raspberry.

"Fine," Vaskel growled. "I was afraid she wouldn't return my feelings. I was afraid she wouldn't want to get involved with a hellkin. We don't have the best reputation for sticking around, you know."

The flutterstoat emitted a sigh that made Vaskel wince.

"I'll admit, it wasn't my bravest moment, but I'd rather battle a mountain troll than risk losing Iris. There's something about her that makes me feel at home, and the way she looks at me makes me feel seen—and not just for my devastating good looks."

Crumpet's groan made Vaskel laugh. Then the flutterstoat chattered something scolding and smacked the side of his head with one of his paws.

"I take your point, and I promise to talk to her once all this is over."

He reached a hand into the pocket of his cloak and felt for the cookie, a comfortable reminder that if everything went according to plan, this would all be over soon.

Taking steady breaths that puffed from his mouth in clouds, he waited for Thrain's sign. That is, until a moan wafted up from below that made the hairs on the nape of his neck stand on end, and Crumpet wrapped his furry arms around Vaskel's head.

Forty-Three

VASKEL STEPPED FARTHER from the castle walls, glancing down at the snow covered ground and attempting to look through Crumpet's arms. The mournful sound had definitely come from beneath him, but he refused to believe it had emanated from the earth itself.

Prying the flutterstoat's arms from his eyes, he held his breath as he listened. The moaning had stopped, leaving only the gentle sounds of rustling underbrush and Crumpet's quick heartbeat in his ears.

"It was nothing," he told himself as much as the flutterstoat. "It was the wind."

Crumpet chittered aggressively, and although Vaskel couldn't interpret his words like Lira did, he was sure the creature was disagreeing with him. But it had to be the wind.

Shaking off the feeling that he was wrong and the winged stoat was right, Vaskel focused on the window he thought belonged to Marina while Crumpet readjusted his position so that he was holding onto Vaskel's horns for balance. Any moment now, Thrain would make a noise that would confirm the room and Crumpet could fly up and let him know when it was time to ingest the cookie and the bind-breaking potion.

Suddenly, his senses prickled to life, and his tail quivered. Almost before he could take a breath, branches snapped behind him and leaves rustled from something that was *not* the wind.

Vaskel pressed himself into a corner of the castle wall where a tower cast a shadow large enough to hide him and Crumpet, drawing his blade from his belt. He held his breath as the whispering underbrush and crunching snow drew closer. Maybe it was a guard on patrol, although given the lax security at the castle, he doubted it. Maybe it was Erindil coming to tell him there was something wrong.

Then a figure emerged from the woods, and Vaskel caught a glimpe of crimson skin. Every muscle in his body stiffened. It was a hellkin. As the cool wash of the moonlight bathed the creature's face, Vaskel's suspicions were confirmed. Not only was it a hellkin, it was a young one. Presumably, a member of Marina's new crew.

As all these things ran through his mind, he tightened his grip on his dagger and prepared to attack if he was spotted. He allowed himself a quiet breath, not daring to move as the hellkin crept along the perimeter of the forest and finally walked toward the castle entrance. Vaskel waited to tuck his blade back under his belt until the hush of the winter night enveloped him once more.

Crumpet patted his head as he moved stealthily away from the castle just enough to peer up at the windows. Had they missed Thrain's signal while they were hiding? He hadn't heard any boisterous dwarf noises, but he'd been more focused on staying hidden than on listening for signals.

His heart pounded as he watched the glow of light spilling from a single window, wishing desperately that he knew what was going on inside. Had the dwarf reached the room, had he found Marina inside, had he convinced her of his heartbreak and desire to win her back, had she taken the bait and accepted the cookies? What would happen if Thrain ran into the other hellkins? If Erindil did?

There were so many questions that doubt started needled its way into Vaskel's mind as the cold seeped into his bones. Even for an infernal being who ran hot, it was cold outside. The longer Vaskel waited in the dark, the more his doubts grew.

"This is taking too long," he whispered, squinting to see a shadow pass in front of the window or really any sign that someone was inside the room.

Crumpet cooed, patting one of Vaskel's horns, which the hellkin found more than a little reassuring.

"Thanks, Crumpet," he said, wondering if he should send the creature up to check on the window.

As he was reminding himself why he didn't want to risk Crumpet yet, the flutterstoat lifted off his head and flapped his furry wings toward the window. So much for caution.

Vaskel thought about calling him back down. The last thing he wanted was for the enchanted creature to be spotted, especially by Marina, but at least Crumpet could tell him if Marina was in the room.

It only took a few seconds for the flutterstoat to reach the windowsill, and he landed daintily and tucked his wings by his side. He pressed his tiny hands to the glass and leaned close as he peered inside. Then he pulled back, turned and shook his head.

Vaskel's shoulders sagged. Marina wasn't there, which meant

that Thrain was somewhere else in the castle looking for her. It also meant he now had no way of knowing when to eat his cookie. Their plan was slipping through his fingers more and more each second.

"Check the other windows," he hissed. "Maybe she's in another room."

Crumpet dutifully flew to each window on the second level of the castle, peeking through the glass and shaking his head every time. Finally, he glided back down and landed softly on Vaskel's shoulder, patting the hellkin on the head.

"It's not your fault, Crump." Vaskel reached up and rubbed the little guy's head. "I was so sure Marina would be in her room."

"She's not."

The voice came from below him, just like the moan had, and it made his blood turn to ice. He now knew exactly where it was coming from because he knew precisely who it was.

Vaskel hadn't heard the raspy voice in a long time, but he'd never forget the voice of the mage who'd been corrupted by dark magic and tried to kill him. The mage was locked in the castle dungeon. The mage who apparently knew about Marina.

Forty-Four

VASKEL SQUATTED, quickly finding the narrow opening in the stone wall that sat at ground level. The faintest flicker of light crept from it, and Vaskel knew he was seeing the glow of a dungeon torch.

A hoarse laugh echoed from below. "You can't hide from me, Vaskel. The scent of brimstone gives you away."

The hellkin cursed under his breath. Every fiber of his being told him to walk away. Nothing good could come of seeing Malek. But how did Malek know about Marina?

"What do you want?" Vaskel asked.

"To help you, of course."

Malek sounded so much like the mage he'd crewed with that the world seemed to shift under Vaskel's feet, rushing him back to the days of planning quests together and sharing meals over campfires. He curled his hands into fists, letting his fingernails bite into his flesh.

Malek wasn't that mage anymore. He hadn't been since dark magic had consumed him. He'd been a stranger since he'd tried to kill his friends.

"Like you helped Pirrin?" Rage trembled Vaskel's voice.

There was a sharp inhalation. "I thought you wanted to know where the female hellkin is, but if I'm mistaken—"

"How do you know her?" Vaskel snapped.

Another laugh crackled through the cold air. "She's clever—and persuasive." Then Malek's voice changed. "But as far as hellkins go, I prefer you."

Now Vaskel laughed, the sound mirthless and brittle.

"I'd much rather talk face to face." Malek's voice grew distant, as if he were walking away from the high dungeon vent. "Come see me and I'll tell you everything you want to know—where you can find Marina and Cali."

Vaskel's heart lurched, and he swallowed a growl begging for release. He'd be a fool to fall for Malek's tricks, but how did Malek know about Marina and that Cali was with her? So far, there was no word from Thrain, and he wasn't even sure where Erindil had gone. As far as he knew, they were both at the mercy of Marina and her hellkin crew.

Without another word and without giving himself any more time to talk himself out of it, Vaskel backed away. He picked his way through the murky undergrowth, his boots squelching as the icy mud sucked them down, until he reached the castle gates.

There was no sign of Erindil or Thrain, and dread slithered down his spine even as he squared his shoulders.

Vaskel reached up and pulled Crumpet from his shoulder. "Your job is done here, little friend. It's time for you to fly home."

The flutterstoat gave a defiant shake of his head, even folding his tiny arms across his chest.

Vaskel's throat was thick as he stared into the creature's luminous black eyes. "I don't know what will happen in there, and I can't promise you'll be safe."

Crumpet curled his paws into wee fists and raised his arms as if preparing for a fight. Vaskel pressed his lips together, not sure if he would laugh or weep.

"Your bravery is unmatched, my friend, but I need you to go back to the tavern. I need you to tell Lira there's trouble." He wasn't sure how much Lira truly understood the animal's chatter, but it was worth a try. "Tell her it's Malek."

Crumpet wrinkled his nose in distaste. He must have remembered their last encounter with the mage. Then he lowered his furry fists and sighed, nodding reluctantly.

Relief surged through Vaskel. At least he wouldn't be responsible for something befalling Lira's beloved baking assistant.

The flutterstoat unfurled his wings and flapped them, hovering in front of Vaskel before flying toward him and throwing his small arms around the hellkin's neck. He gave him a brief squeeze, chattered something that Vaskel understood as a version of 'good luck', and flew away.

Vaskel watched the white silhouette grow more distant and finally get swallowed up by the dark. Then he pivoted back toward the castle and took long strides toward it.

As glad as he was that Crumpet was on his way back to Lira, he felt the absence of the creature as he walked under the portcullis and into the courtyard. Several torches burned around the stone walls, dappling light on the strewn dirt and straw, but there weren't even the handful of guards that they'd encountered last time.

Vaskel stiffened, swinging his head from side to side. Since when was a castle—even a quiet one with an ailing laird—unguarded? He eyed the stairwell leading inside the castle, but Crumpet had already told him that Marina and Thrain weren't up there. It was possible they were in one of the other wings of the castle, but his gut told him he needed to find Malek.

As much as he hated the idea of seeing the mage who'd murdered Pirrin again, he also knew that Malek had information on Marina. Even if he didn't know where she and Cali were, he needed to know how much contact he'd had with the hellkin. He needed to know how much Malek had told Marina about him and their crewing days. He was under no illusion that Malek might very well be leading him into a trap, but he was desperate for information, and Malek knew something.

He curled his hands into fists and readied himself to see the dark mage he'd hoped he'd never have to encounter again. But before he could head to the dungeons, a figure burst from another entrance to the castle.

"I hoped I'd see you again," the hellkin growled as he raced toward Vaskel, his tail slashing behind him.

Vaskel's own tail lashed through the air as he feigned moving to one side, then switched at the last moment, dodging the hellkin and pivoting behind him. He brought a sharp elbow down hard on his attacker's neck, grunting with satisfaction when the hellkin stumbled to his knees.

It wasn't the guy's fault. Vaskel had decades of experience on him and more battles than the young hellkin could imagine, even if he wasn't as young and bloodthirsty anymore. Since the hellkin wasn't using a weapon, Vaskel didn't draw his blade, preferring to dispatch his opponent in hand-to-hand combat.

Before the hellkin could rise, Vaskel leapt up onto its back, using his knees to pin the arms while he hooked one arm around the hellkin's neck. Vaskel held on despite the thrashing and struggling, tightening his grip until the body beneath him slowed and then went limp. When it collapsed to the hard dirt, Vaskel jumped free and landed in a crouch.

Breathing hard, Vaskel glanced around and then took the hellkin by the ankles and dragged him behind a dilapidated cart, kicking some loose straw over him and quelling the urge to flick festering manure on the unconscious figure.

Now he had some idea why there were no guards around. If Marina's hellkin crew was wandering the place, he suspected the guards had been dispatched.

With his senses on high alert, he continued through the courtyard. When he caught another flash of movement from another arched doorway, he let loose a string of hellkin curses. He instinctively stepped back and crouched into a fighting stance to take on the next hellkin—until Thrain rushed out.

He blew out a relieved breath. "Thrain! Where—?"

"No time for small-talk, laddie." Thrain ran to him, his long beard swinging from side to side. "Where's the cookie?"

Vaskel pulled it from hi pocket. "Here, but why—?"

Thrain roughly snatched the cookie and shoved it in Vaskel's mouth mid-sentence. "Sorry, Vask. Open wide."

Thrain's meaty hands covered his lips and muffled Vaskel's mumbled shock. "Mmmpfiggwilskerpiff?"

"You'll thank me later." Thrain gasped, beads of sweat clinging to his forehead. "If I was in time, that is."

Vaskel chewed and swallowed and pulled Thrain's hands from his mouth. "You want to tell me what's going on?"

The dwarf jerked a thumb behind him. "Found Marina, but she wasn't in her room." He put a hand to his side as he winced and gulped another breath. "She was in the great hall. There was no way to signal you. No windows."

He held up a finger as he bent over and continued gasping for air. "Hold on. I ran a lot of stairs." He finally straightened. "I convinced her I was desperate to win her back. I might have even cried a few tears."

Vaskel eyed him, wondering if Thrain had been acting or not.

"The long and short of it is I got her to eat the cookie." The dwarf puffed out his barrel of a chest. "But then I remembered you needed to eat yours and I had no way to signal you so I told her I had the trots and ran to find you." He grinned, his teeth a flash of white nestled in his dark whiskers. "Which I did."

Vaskel took a few seconds to take in Thrain's story. "Do you think she took long enough to eat the cookie, so that we were eating at the same time?"

Thrain shrugged. "Dunno, but I know I ran faster than I ever have before. Couldn't have been more than a couple of minutes, and Marina likes to take her time with food."

Vaskel didn't feel any different, but Erindil had never mentioned what would happen when and if they broke the soul bind. He hadn't expected a flash of lightning, but he would have thought there would be some reaction. His heart sank. Unless he'd been too late.

He shoved up his sleeve, his breath trapped in his throat. The marks were still there. He squinted in the moonlight. But were they lighter? Were they fading, or was it wishful, desperate thinking?

Pushing aside the doubts that threatened to overtake him, he pulled his sleeve over his arm and clapped a hand on Thrain's shoulder. "Thank you, my friend. I couldn't have asked for more."

The dwarf grunted, gripping Thrain's arm. "I wouldn't have told a beautiful woman I had the trots for anyone else."

Vaskel grinned at this before he thought of another question. "Did you see Cali? Was she with Marina?"

Thrain frowned. "She wasn't. I don't know where she is." Another lift of the shoulder. "Maybe Marina has her locked up?"

Would Marina have put Cali in the dungeons with Malek? Was that how Malek knew about the hellkin?

A chill convulsed his body as he thought about Cali at the mercy of Malek. He needed to go down into those dungeons.

"Your job is done here, friend," he said, locking his gaze on the dwarf. "You should get back to the tavern."

"And leave you here?" Thrain shook his head. "We might not have been crew mates like you and Cali, Rog, and Lira were, but that doesn't mean we're any less family."

Vaskel's heart swelled. "Any crew would have been lucky to have you, and you're right, we are family now."

Thrain's grin split his face. "It's settled then. Now, what do you want to do next? Confront Marina? Alert the guards?"

The hellkin tipped his head toward the stone archway that led down. "We're going to the dungeons."

"Argh, spawn of a moldy goblin's knob," the dwarf muttered darkly.

Forty-Five

VASKEL AND THRAIN crossed the courtyard and entered the archway that led to the dungeons, walking in silence through the shadowy corridors. When Vaskel's neck prickled and his tail quivered, he flattened himself against the wall and pulled the dwarf with him.

The shadows hugging the stone walls kept them out of sight until the hellkin was almost on top of them. Vaskel kept his arm across Thrain until the last possible moment, and when the dwarf leapt out, the hellkin fumbled for his blade.

Vaskel used the distraction to slip behind him and fasten the crook of his arm around the fighter's neck, jerking him off his feet before he could grasp his knife or turn.

"Sorry about this, laddie," Thrain whispered as the hellkin's feet danced across the top of the stone floor as he tried to find purchase.

Vaskel squeezed until he lost consciousness and was sure the hellkin would be out for a while. Then he let him slump to the floor.

That was two hellkins he'd taken out without drawing his dagger, but he still hadn't found the important one. "You don't know how many hellkins are in Marina's crew, do you?"

"As far as I know, there are two." Thrain produced a length of twine from one of his pockets. "I'll tie up this one."

"You carry rope?" Vaskel eyed the dwarf and the many layers of leather he wore.

Thrain's teeth flashed white through his whiskers, and he patted his greatcoat. "I carry a lot of things."

Once they tied up the hellkin and shoved him into a murky corner, they continued along the corridor until they found the stairs that coiled down into the earth. Vaskel led the way, keeping his back to the cool, stone wall as he edged down the spiraling steps, his nose twitching with the loamy scent of earth, the fetid odor of mold, and the stink of something rotting.

At the bottom of the stairs, he hesitated long enough for Thrain to catch up and for his eyes to adjust to the dim light. A single undulating flame glowed at the tip of a torch that sagged in an iron sconce.

Vaskel snatched the torch, holding it in front of him to light the way as he walked along the dirt floor and stepped around bleak puddles with the dwarf echoing his path. They passed empty cell after empty cell, the iron bars warped and rusted. Then the back of his neck prickled, and he waved a hand behind him so Thrain would fall back.

Vaskel continued a few more steps until he reached the farthest cell and stopped. His tail lashed behind him as he locked eyes with the mage. His former friend was gaunt with sallow skin stretched tight over sharp bones. Dark lines still crawled like hungry vines beneath his skin. Lines that looked too similar to his own.

"Hello, Malek."

"Vaskel." Malek's sharp features contorted into a malevolent smile. "My old friend. My old crew mate who had me locked away to die."

Each word was like a blade, intended to cut and wound.

Vaskel merely returned the smile, although fury seethed beneath his own placid expression. "You killed Pirrin, and you tried to kill the rest of us. You abandoned your friends for dark magic. You brought this one yourself, old friend."

Malek cringed at this, his smile faltering. "Pirrin was never supposed to die. That was a mistake."

"A mistake?" Vaskel ground out each word, fighting off memories of his ranger friend.

Malek looked down at his hands as if they weren't his own. "The dark magic was too much. I didn't know how to control it. I didn't..."

Vaskel steadied the slashing of his tail as the mage's words died on his lips. He didn't want Malek to know how hard it was to keep from lunging at him through the bars. He also knew he needed the mage for information, which meant he couldn't strangle him. Not yet, at least.

He opened his arms wide. "But you welcomed the dark magic, and here we are."

"Here we are," Malek repeated woodenly, and for a beat he sounded like the old Malek, the one Vaskel had known before dark magic consumed him.

Vaskel reminded himself who he was talking to as he peered through the darkness. "We've all made our choices, haven't we?"

Malek's breathe a sigh that sounded more weary than anything. "You made the choice to come down here."

"You said you know something about Marina and Cali." Vaskel schooled his voice into something approaching civil. "Tell me how you know Marina."

Malek took a step forward, and his chains jangled. Vaskel glanced at the metal that encased the mage's ankles. The shackles were forged from nerillium, which absorbed magical powers, and were the only reason he could face the mage without fear of being hit with a spell.

"I know you never told us about your days running with another hellkin and...was it an orc and a one-eyed dwarf?" Malek fluttered a hand as if brushing away the details. "I know that you did plenty of things for coin that you never would have admitted to when I knew you as the honorable and brave Vaskel."

Heat burned Vaskel's face, but he straightened. He was done hiding his past. Even if it was only Malek and Thrain listening, he wanted to own up to the mistakes he'd made. "All true, but I'm not that hellkin anymore. I left him behind long ago."

"And you think you can do that?" Malek's voice cracked. "Leave darkness behind you and step into light?"

The hellkin narrowed his eyes. Was he imagining things again, or was his old friend asking because he wished to leave his own darkness in the past?

"Are you asking if I believe you can be forgiven for dark deeds?" Vaskel thought about the bounties he'd collected when he'd run with Marina, the treasure he'd stolen, the lives he'd hurt. He swallowed a hot lump of shame. "I believe we all falter, we all make decisions out of fear and hurt. It's what we do after we fall that defines us. It's what we do with the second chance that makes us who we are in the end."

Thrain cleared his throat. "You can't take back the steps you walked, but you can always start a new path forward."

Malek flicked his eyes to the dwarf, and then stared at Vaskel hard, his lips a white line. He dipped his head, finally raising it and meeting Vaskel's gaze. "And you, Vaskel? What have you done with your second chance?"

Vaskel thought of Lira and the others at the tavern. He thought about the villagers in Wayside. He thought about Iris and the way she'd kissed him. Then he thought about Malek and Marina and how both were skilled at manipulation.

"I've made friends I refuse to abandon to a vengeful hellkin or the mage she's convinced to help her."

Malek's black eyes glinted. "You think I'm in league with her?"

The tip of Vaskel's tail vibrated, a sure sign that danger was near. "If you aren't, tell me where she is and where she has Cali."

Malek folded his hands in front of himself, lacing his bony fingers. "Our dear archer is unharmed and here of her own accord, from what I've seen."

Vaskel found it hard to believe that Cali would have seen Malek and not been alarmed that he and Marina were connected. Unless the mage was lying. He still hadn't told Vaskel anything to prove his claims held any truth.

"Then where is she?" Vaskel took a step closer.

Malek tilted his head. "You came here all alone to rescue Cali? You truly have changed. The Vaskel I knew would never do something so foolish."

A shiver passed through Vaskel. It had been a mistake coming to see Malek. It had been a mistake to think he would be any help at all.

He spun on his heel, his cloak flapping around his legs as he turned to go. Strangely, he didn't spot Thrain right away. The dwarf must have hidden in the shadows. "Goodbye, Malek."

"Everyone is in the main hall," Malek said, a note of desperation in his voice. "Marina arranged for a banquet. Everyone is there."

"A banquet?" Vaskel turned. "There hasn't been a banquet at Grayhelm in years. Why would she throw a banquet?"

"To celebrate your return, of course."

The voice that emerged from the shadows near the stairwell was not Malek's.

Marina stepped into view, dressed not in peasant attire but in her usual snug leather. Her inky hair spilled over her shoulders, and light danced across her crimson skin from the flailing torch fire.

"I knew you'd come," she said with a sultry smile directed only to him. Until she slid it to Malek. "See? I told you he'd come."

Malek stepped forward, shaking off the shackles that were not locked around his ankles and pushing open the cell door. "You were right."

Forty-Six

VASKEL LOOKED between Marina and Malek, backing away until they were both in front of him. "I should have known."

His fingers ached to snatch his blade from his belt but if Malek had use of his powers, it would be pointless. Besides, he didn't want them to know he was armed until the last possible moment. Let them be lured into thinking he was more vulnerable than he was.

"You should have." Marina graced him with a look that bordered on pitying. "I stumbled across your old friend shortly after I arrived at the castle, and we both had so many stories to share about you."

"I'm flattered," Vaskel said flatly.

Marina's smile flickered. "He told me all about you and your friends throwing him in here, so I switched out those awful nerillium chains for iron ones. There's no point in having a dark mage on my crew if he can't cast." She made tsking noises in her throat. "The Vaskel I knew wouldn't have been lured so easily. He wouldn't have trusted someone who'd betrayed him."

Vaskel didn't know if she was referring to Malek or herself, but he supposed it didn't matter. She was right. The Vaskel she'd run with wouldn't have trusted anyone. Then again, the old Vaskel wouldn't have been trustworthy either. He wouldn't have given grace because he had received none. But now he had. Now he had friends he trusted with his life and friends who accepted him, flaws and all.

"I'm not the Vaskel you knew."

Marina eyed him, considering this. Then she shrugged. "You're still a hellkin with the power to sense danger and the ability to charm almost anyone. You're still a valuable asset."

Vaskel saw no trace of Cali with Marina. He hoped that meant she was safe at the banquet upstairs. Maybe Erindil was getting her out as they spoke. If the elf hadn't encountered Marina's hellkin crew, that is.

"Where's Cali?" he asked once he knew his voice wouldn't betray him.

"It's sweet how you care about this new crew of yours." Marina's smile slipped.

"I'm here," he told her. "You have no need for her anymore."

Marina put a hand to the side of her face and tapped one finger against her cheek. "But she adores me so. It will be hard to let her go."

Vaskel gritted his teeth, thinking about how the hellkin must have sweet-talked the pantheri, convincing her of her undying affection. He'd seen Marina do it enough to know exactly what she would have said and done. He was only sad he wouldn't be around to help Cali nurse her damaged heart.

"But you will let her go," Vaskel said, steel edging his voice. "Or I won't go with you."

She laughed. "You can't fight the soul bind."

Vaskel touched a hand to his arm. He couldn't risk a peek, but his skin no longer burned like the marks were writhing to sear their way through his flesh. It was almost too much to believe that Thrain had reached him on time and that the bind was broken, but he wanted to believe it was true.

"I can't be bound to you if I'm no longer alive," he snarled.

This made her smile drop and her eyes harden. "I don't like threats like that."

"Then you'll let my friends go," he said. "All of them."

Marina huffed out a breath as if he were being a petulant child. "Fine. Your friends aren't the ones I wanted, anyway."

"What about Malek?" Vaskel asked. "You've freed him."

Marina flashed a grin at the dark mage. "You've been most helpful. I couldn't have done any of this quite as effectively without you. Your insight into my old friend and his crew was invaluable. I hope you enjoy your freedom from those stifling chains."

Vaskel's pulse raced at the thought of Malek going free with Wayside so close. "He's not joining your crew?"

"*Our* crew," corrected Marina. "It's up to him. Our deal was information for freedom. He gave me what I needed to know about your friends, and I released him from his cell. I would never renege on a deal."

Something niggled at the back of his brain. "Malek here might have helped you with information, but how did you know he was here? How did you know I was here?"

Marina rubbed her hands together as if savoring the answer. "I suppose there's no harm in telling you now. I encountered the most fascinating character as I was assembling my new crew. The old man was staying at the tavern where we were, and he was clearly nursing a grudge. It didn't take more than a few ales to get the truth from him and discover the source of his ire."

Vaskel didn't respond.

"Silas, I think his name was," Marina said. "He told me all about the sick laird, the barely defended castle, and the charming nearby village hosting a recently arrived hellkin. A hellkin and his meddling friends who ruined his favorite tavern, if I've got the story right."

Vaskel barely remembered an old man named Silas, but a lot had changed since Lira had come to Wayside and welcomed her friends. Changes for the good, if you asked most folks.

Vaskel attempted a charming smile. "You can't win them all."

Marina laughed. "Not my philosophy."

Marina waved Vaskel toward her. "We should go. The banquet will keep the castle distracted for a while, especially since I've plied the guards with plenty of whiskey, but I want to be far away when they realize I'm gone."

"Why?" Vaskel asked. "What have you done?"

Marina flicked her wrist in a circle. "I promised to cure the laird, but there's no cure for decrepitude."

Vaskel flinched at the hellkin's casual dismissal. "You haven't changed a bit, Marina."

She twitched, a sneer replacing her silky smile. "Not everyone wants to change, Vaskel."

"But everyone can," he said, more to Malek than to her. "Like my dwarf friend says, every new tunnel forges a fresh path ahead."

Neither Thrain nor Sass had never actually said that, but it sounded dwarfy enough.

Marina groaned. "Enough with the pointless dwarf wisdom."

Thrain leapt from the shadows, placing himself between Marina and Vaskel. "What are you calling pointless?"

Marina's brows lifted ever so slightly. "What happened to your undying love for me? You were offering me gifts not so long ago, little man."

"I'm no man." Thrain bristled, a low growl rumbling in his chest. "I'm the hells-cursed dwarf here to tell you that you're not taking my friend."

"This is so tiresome." Marina's face contorted into something that was more demon than woman. "I suppose I need to show your dwarf friend what happens to those who fight a soul bind."

She exposed her own wrist, pressing a finger to the flesh and giving Vaskel a malevolent grin. Nothing happened. Her grin faltered, and she dropped her gaze to her arm. "What? Where?" She yanked the fabric up to reveal nothing but fiery, unmarked skin. Then she shot Vaskel a look of pure venom. "How did you—?"

"Wasn't him," Thrain bellowed. "'Twas me."

Marina swung to Thrain, and for a moment, Vaskel was certain the hellkin was going to lunge for him. Instead, she ground her teeth and spun on one heel. "Hells take you all."

"One thing before you go, Marina." Malek extended his hands, the palms fiery and vibrating.

Vaskel instinctively dove for Thrain, tackling the dwarf and covering his body with his own as a blast rattled his teeth and a blinding light illuminated the entire dungeon. Vaskel's ears rang as dust and shards of rock rained down onto his back.

When he rolled off the dwarf and pulled Thrain upright, Marina lay on the ground motionless, and Malek had crumpled to his knees.

"Is she dead?" Vaskel whispered, almost afraid to ask.

Malek twisted his head to lock eyes with him. "No, but her powers are gone, along with any chance for her to bind another soul."

"Why?" Vaskel asked.

"I'm not so far gone that I didn't see through her or know she was using me to get to you." He swayed as he glowered at the hellkin on the ground. "I suppose I don't like it when someone thinks they've outsmarted me." He held up his pale arms that were scored with black marks. "And a part of me hoped that if I used my powers for good, maybe there was still hope for me to sever the darkness trying to devour me."

Vaskel's neck prickled, a warning that had nothing to do with Malek, who appeared truly depleted as he listed from side to side. It was Marina who pushed herself back onto her feet, her teeth bared.

"You're a fool if you think you can be redeemed," she spat out, her gaze shifting between Malek and Vaskel, "both of you."

Then she whipped out a dagger from her waistband. Vaskel didn't think before diving for her, his arm knocking hers as she released the blade at Malek.

The knife spun off-course and clanged into a stone wall, drawing a screech from Marina, who rounded on Vaskel. All pretense of friendship was gone, replaced only by a look of pure spite.

"You've ruined everything," she cried, lunging for him hands like claws.

Vaskel snatched her hands with his and whirled her around, curling an arm around her neck and using another to pin her arms to her side. He tightened his grip around her neck as she flailed, holding her until her movements slowed and she slumped in his grasp.

"Is she...?" Thrain asked.

Vaskel shook his head as he lowered her to the ground. "Just incapacitated." As much as he would have liked to never have to worry about Marina again, he refused to be a killer. Never again.

A part of him knew that if he spilled blood, even for a justifiable reason, he would ruin everything he'd worked so hard to build in Wayside.

"You saved me." The voice was shaky and the tone surprised.

Vaskel lifted his gaze to Malek, giving the mage a small nod.

Just as he refused to let Marina make him a killer, he refused to let Malek make him heartless.

The mage dredged up a watery smile before collapsing onto the ground.

Thrain rushed forward, bending down and putting a finger to Malek's neck. "Not dead."

Footsteps echoed in the stairwell, and Vaskel braced himself for the appearance of guards or perhaps more hellkins. Instead, Erindil emerged from the stairwell, his gaze darting first to the inert hellkin and then to Malek, Thrain, and Vaskel. Then another figure descended the stairs behind him, and Vaskel's jaw dropped.

Two elves?

Forty-Seven

"THERE YOU ARE, DEAR BOY." Erindil stepped over Marina as if she were a misplaced throw pillow. "I've been looking for you, you know." His gaze alighted on Thrain, and he blew out a breath. "And you too. I was certain I'd lost you both."

"Where have you been?" Vaskel fought to keep the sharpness from his voice, but he was too distracted by the presence of a second, regal elf to be too upset. "And who is that?

"As to where I was," Erindil allowed himself a satisfied smile. "I was tracking down our missing archer. You see, I saw Marina walking without her and deduced that Cali must be hidden away somewhere, perhaps subdued. I was conducting a search of the castle while all this was going on." He fluttered his fingers in the general direction of the dungeon and the prone hellkin. "As to who this is..." He pivoted to the other elf who looked like a slightly younger, and considerably less fussy, version of him. "This is my nephew."

Everyone in the dank dungeon stared at the elf, and the only sound accompanying the shock was the plinking of water on stone.

"You mean," Vaskel's words tripped from his lips, "this is Lira's...?"

"Older brother," Erindil said, then tapped a finger on his chin. "Yes, older. Sometimes the years get a bit muddled."

The elf with long platinum blonde hair and green eyes that were a perfect match for Lira's slid an amused glance to Erindil. "I am two hundred years older than Lira." Then he shifted his gaze back to Thrain and Vaskel and dipped his head as if he'd been formally introduced. "I am Tarrel."

Instead of the fur-lined robes like his uncle, Tarrel wore forest-green pants that hugged his legs and a matching tunic that almost reached his knees. Brown leather encased his forearms, and a dark cloak draped over his shoulders. He looked more like a ranger than an immortal from Lananore.

Then Thrain barked out a laugh. "It's you I've been seeing and thinking it was Erindil."

Suddenly Vaskel's own sighting of Erindil in odd clothing made sense.

Tarrel's lips quirked almost imperceptibly. "I have been watching Wayside and my sister, sometimes not as unseen as I might have liked."

Erindil narrowed his eyes at his nephew. "You've caused lots of confusion, is what you've done. I've had villagers thinking I'm vaporizing and reappearing."

Tarrel's gaze swept over Erindil. "They've been mistaking me for you?"

"Yes." Erindil sniffed. "Just because I don't dress like I'm living off the land doesn't mean we don't share similarities."

"You *do* look alike." Thrain chuckled. "I'm just glad there are two of you, and it's not the ale that was getting to me."

Vaskel scowled at Tarrel, his protectiveness of Lira flaring. "Why haven't you made yourself known to Lira?"

The elf blinked slowly. "I was waiting for the right moment."

"The right moment? How long have you known about her?"

"Since she was young, I suppose." The elf's placid brow wrinkled. "But decades are a blink of an eye to an elf."

Thrain huffed out a breath and muttered some unflattering words about elves under his breath so only Vaskel could hear him.

"Well, your sister is all grown up," Vaskel said. "While you were blinking your eyes, she grew up without parents or siblings, lost the gran who raised her and set out on her own to make something of herself, which she did. Now she's built a life and a home and is about to get married."

"That's right," Thrain added. "So don't think you can waltz in like no time has passed."

Erindil shifted from one foot to the other, flitting glances at his nephew. "I told Tarrel that humans might not understand the way we move through time." The elf lowered his voice to a conspiratorial whisper. "He's not as grounded in the ways of the greater world as I am."

Vaskel didn't imagine that there could be a creature less grounded than Erindil with his ornate robes and battle ostrich.

"I have no intention of causing trouble," Tarrel said, his voice smooth and unflustered. "I merely heard talk of a hellkin crew in Wayside and wanted to keep an eye on things."

"You heard about Marina's crew?" Vaskel asked.

Tarrel nodded. "I overheard her talking to an old man in a

tavern. It was clear that she didn't have good intentions, so I followed her and her fellow hellkins."

"Wait." Vaskel held up a hand. "You've been here this whole time?"

"He has." Erindil's smile slipped, and he looked down his long nose at Tarrel. "He didn't alert me to his presence, either, although there is plenty of room in my encampment. And don't say you're too good for my tents." Erindil waved a hand at his nephew's attire. "I see how you're dressed."

Unless Vaskel was mistaken, Tarrel actually rolled his eyes. Maybe elf families weren't so different after all.

"Hold up," Thrain said, wagging a finger in Erindil's direction. "You said you were looking for Cali? Where is she?"

The elf's face drooped. "I didn't find her. Of course, I hadn't searched every corner of the castle before I stumbled into my nephew. Then we heard the explosion down here and came running."

Vaskel swore quietly. He couldn't return without Cali.

"I can search room by—" Thrain started, but his words were cut off by a yowl from a corner of the dungeon that was dredged in shadows.

"Cinders and dragon dung. Where am I?"

Vaskel would know that voice anywhere. "Cali?"

The pantheri ambled into the light, her fur rumpled and her whiskers bent. She eyed the rust-flaked iron bars in front of her, then her black pupils grew even larger as she peered beyond the bars to the assemblage in the dungeon. "What in Grognick's beard is going on?"

Malek roused himself from the ground, giving a shake of his head as he sat up cross-legged. "Ah yes. I suppose now is the time to tell you that Caliqua has been here all along."

Vaskel shot a dark look at the mage. "You couldn't have mentioned that sooner?"

Malek twitched a shoulder. "She was fine, and it didn't suit me to reveal her whereabouts right away."

Thrain swiveled his head, spied a hook on one wall with a ring of keys, yanked it down, and hurried to the cell door. "Good to see you again, Cal." He jammed a key in the crusty lock, pulled open the door, and held it for her. "No hard feelings about Marina or about the duel we almost fought."

"What?" Cali rubbed her head. "We almost fought a duel?"

Vaksel put an arm around her shoulders, ignoring Thrain. "You okay?"

The pantheri gave a slow, deliberate nod of her head, then her gaze landed on the unmoving form of Marina. "She's trouble." She shook a raised claw in her direction. "I almost fell for her too, but I overheard her talking about her plans for her new crew. I wanted no part of that."

"I thought you missed adventure," Vaskel said.

"I might miss our old adventures, but I realized that I can't recapture that by joining a new crew, especially not one bent on trouble." Cali curled her tail around the hellkin's leg. "My forever crew is right here in Wayside."

Vaskel cleared the lump in his throat. "I'm glad to hear you say that. I would have knocked you out and dragged you back to the village, but I prefer this way."

"Me, too." The pantheri shook out her whiskers. "I'm ready to get out of here. Unless there's a reason we're all hanging out in the dungeon."

"There is the matter of the hellkin and the mage." Erindil said.

Cali bristled when she spotted Malek outside his cell, the hairs on her arms puffing up. "What in the—?"

Vaskel put a hand on one fluffy arm. "He's actually the one who knocked out Marina."

"And siphoned her powers from her," Malek added.

"What?" Cali turned to face the mage fully. "Are you trying to redeem yourself after trying to kill your crew?"

Malek flinched but met Vaskel's eyes. "I've been told that everyone deserves a second chance."

While Cali grumbled, Vaskel held Malek's gaze, searching hard for signs of deception but finding none.

"If I might," Tarrel said. "The mage still carries dark magic within him. Dark magic is hard to resist repeatedly unless it can be removed."

Erindil whipped his head toward his nephew. "Do you think...?"

"I do." Tarrel eyed Malek, then gave a curt bob of his head. "I will take him myself."

Vaskel bit back a sigh at the mysterious elves and their even more enigmatic conversation. "Do you mind telling us?"

"Of course, dear boy." Erindil rubbed his hands together. "Tarrel is offering to take Malek to Lananore where the elves can treat him and cleanse his soul of the dark magic."

Malek bowed his head. "I would be grateful."

"What about Marina?" Thrain asked, "We can't exactly leave her and her hellkin crew to keep causing trouble."

Vaskel slid up his sleeve, swallowing a shaky breath when he confirmed that there was nothing there but smooth, crimson flesh. The soul bind was gone. Even if Marina were free, she would have no more power over him. He'd also gotten his second chance.

Erindil's face brightened, and he bounced on the balls of his feet. "I have an idea."

Forty-Eight

VASKEL HELPED Korl heave Marina's still-unconscious body into the back of the wooden cart beside the two young hellkins Vaskel had knocked out earlier and stepped back.

"Where are we taking them again?" Val asked as they gathered around Vorto and Klaff's cart in the dark. The blacksmith workshop remained quiet, as did the rest of Wayside.

"The nearest port town is Eldu," Erindil said. "You should find a ship looking for sailors. Some of them won't ask questions."

"Best if you pick a ship with a long, dangerous voyage ahead of them," Thrain added. "With any luck, those two won't wake until there's nothing but open water and sea monsters."

Korl hefted himself onto the buckboard, and Val followed, but not before Sass, Iris, and Lira came running from the tavern. Crumpet rode Lira's shoulder with his fluffy tail curled around her neck for balance.

"Wait," Lira called out, slowing to a stop when she reached the wagon. "Where are you going?"

"Your charming fiancé and his burly friend are taking our prisoners to Eldu," Erindil said.

Lira peered into the back of the cart, her eyes widening at the sight of the hellkins.

Sass huffed up behind, complaining loudly about her shorter legs. When she spotted Thrain, she threw her arms around him. "You're alive, and you didn't fall under that she-beast's spell again."

Thrain patted her gruffly. "Course I didn't. I saved Vaskel, didn't I? Helped break the bind."

Sass pulled back. "Did you now?"

Vaskel pushed up his sleeve to reveal his unmarked arm.

"It worked!" Lira clapped her hands. "I can't believe it actually worked."

"I can't either," Iris whispered. She was hanging back, her eyes not quite willing to meet Vaskel's yet.

"I beg your pardon, ladies." Erindil drew himself up to his full height. "You doubted my potion?"

"Aye, let's be fair." Sass flipped her dark braid behind her shoulder. "Potion in a cookie seemed like a long shot."

Even Vaskel laughed along with the rest of the group at that. It had been a long shot, and it had only worked because of the efforts of everyone working together to help him. He doubted he could ever repay them all.

"You should get going." Erindil said once the laughter faded. "They might be tied up, but we don't want them waking up on the way."

Lira hurried over to Korl, and he bent down to kiss her, dark splotches on his green cheeks evident even with only the moon for light. Sass hurried to Val's side of the wagon, giving the guardswoman a kiss that wasn't nearly as shy as Korl's.

In the flurry of the reins being jiggled and the horses being urged on, Iris stepped closer to Vaskel. "I'm glad you're rid of the soul bind, but I wanted to apologize for my enthusiasm earlier."

He tilted his head at her. "You mean the kiss?"

Her cheeks mottled, and she flicked her fingers through the curls near her temple. "Yes, well, I might have gotten swept up in the moment, but—"

Vaskel wrapped an arm around her waist, pulling her flush to him as he curled his tail around her legs. "Then consider this me getting swept up in another moment." Then he crushed his mouth to hers, pouring all his feelings, all his suppressed longing, all his desire into a kiss.

When he finally pulled away, Iris blinked heavily at him. "Oh, my."

"Unless you have any objections, I plan to get swept up with you much more in the future," he husked.

Her chest hitched, and she lifted a hand to his head and ran her fingers along the ridges of his horn before tangling in his hair. "I have no objections."

Vaskel was about to pull the apothecary into another kiss when he realized he could no longer hear the flapping of reins or the creaking of the cart's wheels. He turned to find that the cart had rolled off down the road and over the bridge, and all their friends were gaping at them.

Iris giggled. "Maybe we should continue this discussion in my shop?"

Vaskel knew he should probably debrief with everyone and spend more time thanking all his friends. He also knew it could wait a few hours. They would understand.

He took Iris by the hand and tugged her toward the village. "I think we should."

Forty-Nine

"LOOK WHAT THE GOBLINS DRAGGED IN!" Thrain thunked his tankard on the bar when he spotted Vaskel slinking in the tavern door the next morning.

Vaskel had hoped that the place would be empty, but it appeared that no one had retired for the night.

Sass lay sprawled across the arms of Val's armchair by the cold fire while Cali was curled up in the chair across from hers. The dwarf startled at the sound of Thrain's booming voice. "What? Who? Are they back yet?"

"Not yet," Thrain said, turning on his barstool to face the hearth. "It's just Vaskel returning from his lady love's."

Part of Vaskel wanted to groan, but another part of him very much liked the sound of that. Iris was his love, after all, and it felt wonderful not to hide that anymore. It had been more wonderful to stay up talking with her in her back room, with her cuddled on his lap on one of her overstuffed chairs as the bookwyrms slept and the snow fell.

Cali opened one eye, then closed it and wrapped her arms over her head to block out any light.

"Why are you back, anyway?" Thrain blinked bleary eyes at him.

"I wanted to let Iris get some sleep, and I wanted to check on Lira. I'm assuming that she's heard about her brother by now?"

Sass waved a hand toward the back of the tavern. "She's with him and Erindil at the encampment. They've been talking all night."

Vaskel glanced at the door that led behind the tavern to the collection of elf tents and beyond that to the stream. "Do you think she's okay?"

"Well, she did just learn that her elf brother, whom she's never met, has been stalking her." Sass shrugged. "The upside is that she'll probably work through all this by baking."

Thrain leaned back and peered over his beard at Sass. "Are you happy that our friend's trauma will benefit our bellies?"

Sass wiggled her way out of the chair. "I'm not unhappy I'll get to test more types of scones and maybe a cake or two." She leveled a finger at Thrain. "When your heart gets broken, all we get is a dent in our ale stores."

Thrain spluttered at that as Vaskel made his way to the bar. The kitchen was quiet, and he imagined that Crumpet and Bramble were still sleeping soundly in the nests of dishrags that Lira had made for them. Even the raccoon had taken to staying in the tavern overnight, and Vaskel wondered how many other woodland creatures would eventually make their home inside the Tusk & Tail.

He walked behind the bar and leaned his hands on the buffed wood. It was the same bar it had always been and the same tavern he worked at every night, but it felt different now. He felt different.

Grinning, he started inspecting the glasses and tankards and was soon humming.

"Is that what I think it is?" Thrain asked. "Are you humming one of Sass's sea shanties?"

Vaskel stopped and thought about it. "I guess I am." He chuckled. "They're catchy."

Sass was beaming as she joined them at the bar, tying on her apron to start the day. "That's what I'm saying."

"A dwarf singing sea shanties." Thrain shook his head. "It's wrong is what it is."

Vaskel had just resumed his humming when Lira walked in through the back door. They all stopped what they were doing and watched her walk to the bar and slide onto a stool.

"Drink?" Vaskel asked, although it was still early in the morning.

Lira nodded wordlessly as Sass hopped onto the stool next to her. Even Cali uncurled from the upholstered chair and walked over, taking the stool on Lira's other side.

Vaskel pulled her a pint and slid it across the bar to her, where she curled her hands around the cool pewter but didn't drink.

"He's leaving with Malek." Lira didn't have to say who.

"Aye." Sass patted Lira's arm. "Are you okay?"

The half-elf loosed a heavy sigh, then sat up straighter. "I think I am. We spent a long time talking. Our father wasn't around much for his childhood either, so I guess we have a few things in common." She managed a smile. "That's actually why he's been traveling around the Known Lands. He's looking for our father."

"And now he's taking Malek back to Lananore," Thrain said.

Lira nodded. "He won't stay there for long though, which means he'll be back here." She smirked. "And I made him promise not to wait a decade to come back. I told him he's on human time, not elf time."

"Wonder what it would have been like to grow up in the elf city," Vaskel said. "It's supposed to be so beautiful you can lose days just staring."

Lira shrugged. "That might be true, but there's still no place I'd rather be than here with all of you."

Cali put a paw on top of one of Lira's hands. "Same."

Thrain sniffled and swiped a hand across his eyes. "Enough of that now."

They all laughed and blinked away tears. Lira glanced up and met Vaskel's eyes. "You broke the soul bind, I met my brother, and Iris finally got a stubborn hellkin to admit that he's crazy about her. Not bad for a night's work."

Vaskel's face warmed, and his mouth fell open. "Wh—how long have you known?"

Cali dropped her head on the bar, rolling it to eye Vaskel. "Soooooooo long."

"I'm glad I got to see it happen before I died," Sass said, and the others nodded in agreement.

Now Vaskel laughed. "Well, I'm happy I finally admitted it, too."

"But if anyone needs powders or tonics," Cali said, "Vaskel has an impressive stash of them."

When he gaped at her, the pantheri shrugged. "Iris told me you were her best customer. I decided not to inform her that hellkins rarely get sick. You're welcome."

"I wonder if she'd take some of those back," Vaskel said. "They've started to take up too much space in my room."

Sass winked at him. "I'll bet she'll do anything you ask her to do if you kiss her like you did last night."

Thrain pounded his hand on the bar as he roared with laughter.

"Let's go easy on Vask," Lira said.

"That's right." Cali nudged her friend. "You're about to be a honeymooner. I guess you're the next to be teased."

Lira slid off her stool, leaving her ale untouched and heading for the kitchen. "I won't be a honeymooner until after our second wedding."

She disappeared through the swinging doors, and the rest of the group exchanged confused glances.

"Did she say second wedding?" Cali asked.

Sass hopped off her stool. "She hasn't even had the first."

Vaskel led the way as they followed Lira into the kitchen. "What's this about a second wedding? I'm assuming you haven't found a second groom."

Crumpet and Bramble were clambering from their nests and stretching as Lira poured milk and spices into a pot for chai and chuckled. "Hardly. My brother wants me to have a second wedding in Lananore so the rest of my family can be there. You're all invited, of course."

Just then the kitchen doors flew open and a pile of burgundy fabric waddled into the room. A pile of fabric with a gnome face protruding from the top.

"No talk about a second wedding until we make it through the first one," Tin said from beneath the fabric. "Have you seen the snow out there? Fenni says a blizzard is heading toward us."

"A blizzard?" Lira almost fumbled the bottle of milk. "The day before my wedding?"

Sass squinted at the window, where the snow was indeed cascading from the sky. "Do you remember how you said you wouldn't mind getting married in front of the tavern fireplace with just us?"

"It still sounds perfect," Lira said as she stirred the warming chai.

Vaskel took in the cozy kitchen and his friends gathered in it, and he drank in the aroma of cinnamon and cardamom. It was moments like these he loved even more than all the epic quests.

Like warm chai on a wintery day, joy comes in sips, not gulps.

CALI TUGGED at the claret-colored vest that topped a matching pair of pants, grateful that she'd been spared the torture of wearing a dress for Lira's wedding. Although she hadn't been spared the task of being a bridal attendant, which required that she leave her bow and quiver of arrows behind.

Her tail twitched uneasily. After being knocked unconscious and dumped in a dungeon cell, she would have preferred to go through the rest of her life well-armed. She shifted on the tavern barstool and tried to suppress thoughts of her time with Marina and how foolish she'd been. No matter how many times Vaskel assured her that many had fallen for Marina's ploys before, embarrassment and shame still made her whiskers pinch.

At least her foolishness hadn't resulted in anyone from Wayside getting hurt or the wedding being postponed. Cali had never been so happy to be at The Tusk & Tail in her life. Or at a wedding, for that matter.

It helped that the place had been buffed and polished to within an inch of its life, thanks to Sass. The long wooden tables were draped in off-white linen, and runners of greenery wound down the centers of them with flowers bursting forth in colorful clusters interspersed with chunky candles sheathed in glass. Even the wrought-iron chandeliers dangling from the rafters boasted swags of greens.

The fire was crackling in the hearth, but stacks of logs burned instead of chunks of peat, giving the great room a pleasant smell— wood smoke mixed with greenery and prodigious amounts of lemon cleaner.

Pip fussed with the wedding cake at a round table near the front door, placing a sprig of greenery around the five-tier confection covered in fluffy white icing before stepping back to admire his work.

"Looks good enough to eat," Cali called out.

Pip jumped and spun around, pressing a small hand to his chest. "Bless the stars! You're so quiet, I forgot you were there."

Cali grinned at him. As grateful as she was for being saved from the dungeon, she was more grateful that none of the villagers knew that she'd considered running off with a hellkin crew. Her friends that did know, had not held it against her.

She thought about what Vaskel had said to her. "If I wasn't your friend through thick and thin, I wouldn't be much of a friend."

She was lucky to have found such friends and such a home, even if she did crave adventure—or at least something to do.

Before she could dwell for too long on her need for purpose, Tinpin hurried through the back door, clapping his wool-encased hands together.

"It's hopeless," he cried, stomping snow from his boots. "Hopeless, I tell you."

He threw off his snow-dusted coat and tossed it onto the nearest barstool, revealing a smart maroon suit expertly crafted from velvet. An ivory ascot was held in place by a glittering garnet stickpin in the shape of a flower. Naturally, the haberdasher had dressed to match the wedding.

"What's hopeless?" Cali asked.

Tin flailed a hand in the general direction of outdoors. "The blizzard is making it impossible to hold the ceremony outside. Impossible! Not even Erindil's warming charm can keep the guests from freezing under a tent. Not to mention that the snow is coming down so heavily you can't even see the stream."

Pip wrung his hands. "Does that mean there won't be a wedding? Will they not need a cake?"

"Or cheese?" Fenni added as he emerged from the tavern kitchen, gaining him a perplexed look from the gnome.

Tin then seemed to notice that Pip was standing next to the towering cake that was taller than all three of them. The gnome pressed a hand to his chest. "It's spectacular, Pip. Truly spectacular. Wayside has never seen one so beautiful."

Pip flushed from the compliment. "But if there won't be a wedding—"

"Nonsense." Sass hurried inside behind Tin with Val and Thrain close at her heels. "Weddings aren't about the fripperies or the fancy clothes. They're about the two people getting married."

Tin grumbled at this, but not loud enough for anyone to hear. After all, fripperies and fancy clothes were his trade.

"A blizzard isn't enough to stop a bride, just like stone isn't enough to stop a pickaxe," Sass added.

"Are you comparing me to a pickaxe?" Lira asked as she walked down the back stairs, a cloak covering her dress beneath.

"You should be flattered," Thrain said. "Dwarves love our axes."

"Aye." Sass winked at Lira. "I've even named axes before."

Cali understood this, since she once had a bow named Clawsong.

"If the ceremony can't be in the tent," Pip asked, "then where—?"

"Why right here, of course," Vaskel said as he and Rog gusted inside with a fair amount of snow flurries. "All we have to do is push back the tables and the ceremony can take place in front of the hearth."

"What about the swaths of gossamer fabric I had draped inside the tent?" Tin asked, his voice rising an octave. "What about the bows on the backs of the chairs?"

"What about the wedding arch?" A deep voice rumbled from the front doorway where Klaff and Vorto stood just outside, carrying the enormous wrought-iron structure between them.

Vaskel crossed the great room to assist, tilting his head as he assessed the massive arch. "Is it possible to bring it in sideways?"

The orcs grunted and maneuvered it onto its side, then Thrain and Rog took the front bars while the orcs pushed from the back. Bit by bit, it wiggled through the door along with the pair of orcs.

Sass stood with her hands braced on her hips as the group straightened the iron arch and placed it on the floor to give everyone a moment to catch their breath. "It's certainly orc-sized."

"I suppose I can drape some fabric on that," Tin muttered, looking slightly mollified.

Iris hurried inside behind the iron arch, rubbing her arms and stamping the snow off her boots. The apothecary pulled a basket packed with fresh flowers and greenery from beneath her cloak. "I barely made it here with these."

Cali slid off the barstool and hurried to Iris, helping her shed her heavy cloak. "I was worried the storm would keep you away. Much longer, and I was going to come fetch you myself."

Iris smiled at her. "Not even a blizzard could keep me away from this wedding."

Cali didn't miss the shy look the apothecary gave Vaskel or the smoldering one he returned to her. Her own grin widened. It was nice to see her friends happy, although Vaskel being a one-woman hellkin would take some getting used to.

Sass waved Iris over. "There's still time for us to whip up a bouquet."

As Cali hung Iris's cloak on a peg by the door and Iris, Sass, and Lira busied themselves with the flowers, Erindil glided through the back door along with his lute player and his ostrich, who was decked out in a splendid harness of burgundy velvet with jeweled reins.

"A bird in the tavern?" Sass said in a stage whisper.

The elf sniffed and lifted his chin. "Glen is the ring bearer."

No one could deny that Glen was dressed for the occasion.

The tavern door flew open again, and Rosie entered with a bottle of brandy under each arm and so much snow on her she resembled a snowman.

"There's no getting through that storm," the gnome said, shaking out her blonde hair and sending ice crystals scattering to the floor to melt. "I only made it because our wagon is a few steps away. None from the village are going to make it."

Lira looked up from tying a bouquet. "What about Korl?"

"I'm here," a gruff voice emanated from a dark corner of the tavern. "I didn't think we were supposed to see each other before the ceremony."

Lira laughed. "I suppose you're right. I'll hide in the kitchen until we're ready."

As she and Iris decamped to the kitchen, Tin fussed with the iron arch, tying fabric bows and draping sheer burgundy fabric down the sides.

Rosie ambled to the bar and handed Vaskel the brandy. "Guess it's just us then."

"Looks perfect to me." Vaskel eyed the small group and smiled. "It only takes a few candles to bring light."

Rosie grinned at him. "You're getting wise on me, Vaskel."

"The years should be good for something."

She let out a belly laugh as she walked away to help Rog arrange the tavern benches into two makeshift aisles. Erindil directed his lute player to a stool where he started to strum, and then the elf beckoned for the men to line up at the back near the bar.

"Wait!" the elf cried. "The woodland fey who was going to perform the ceremony isn't here."

"The blizzard must have waylaid him." Vorto cast a mournful look at the white-out through the windows.

"No worries." Rosie strode to the front. "While Rog was out adventuring, I stayed at a gnome monastery for a spell. Got myself ordained as a cleric of the Church of the Holy Gnome."

Cali and Vaskel exchanged a look, but they both shrugged. It sounded official enough.

"Then we're in luck." Erindil clapped his hands as he led Glen to the back, and the few who weren't processing down the short aisle took their seats on the benches.

After a few minutes of shuffling in the back, Erindil clapped his hands more sharply, and the lute music changed as Vaskel, Rog, Thrain, and Val walked down wearing matching burgundy suits. Korl followed them arm-in-arm with his two dads, also in burgundy, who were both fighting back tears.

Another clap from Erindil, who'd become a stand-in wedding coordinator, and the music changed. The kitchen doors opened and Iris and Sass walked in single file, each wearing a dress made from layers of sheer claret-colored fabric that matched Cali's suit. The pantheri slipped in behind them, processing up the aisle and taking her place to one side of the arch and between Iris and Sass.

Cali tried not to fidget as she stood looking out at the small gathering. She couldn't help grinning at Tin, who was already dabbing at his eyes.

Finally, there was some jostling and fierce muttering in the back before Glen high-stepped his way down the aisle, his saddle jingling. The ostrich didn't look left or right, but kept his head held high. When he reached the front, he marched right up to the iron wedding arch and began munching on one of Tin's bows.

"Glen!" A shriek from the back of the aisle made Glen drop the sodden bow and sink petulantly onto the floor with a mournful sigh.

"That went much better than I expected," Sass said, even as she frowned at the wet bow lying on the floor.

The lute player paused, and his tempo quickened, the music suddenly dramatic as Lira began her walk down the aisle on her uncle Erindil's arm. Her dress was a silky white creation that draped over her curves and flowed in gossamer layers behind her, making her look as beautiful and ethereal as any elf. A veil draped over her auburn hair, which she wore in loose curls, and she carried a bouquet of flowers, berries, and greenery tied with bakery twine.

For once, Erindil's outfit was relatively subdued. His dark suit was exquisitely tailored but simple. The only nod to his personality or the wedding colors was the immense ruby brooch on his lapel.

Cali's eyes stung with tears as she watched one of her dearest friends walk down the aisle. She'd never expected to become emotional, but the pantheri was struck by the sweetness of the moment and also by how close she felt to everyone in the tavern. Lira wasn't just her friend. She was her family. As was Vaskel and Rog and now Iris and Sass and all the villagers she'd come to love.

Lira didn't notice her tear-filled eyes, though. She didn't glance at her attendants or at the friends seated on the benches or even at her uncle. Her eyes were locked on Korl, who was grinning helplessly, a single tear trailing down his face.

Tin produced a floral handkerchief and blew his nose loudly

into it as Pip patted him on the arm. Vorto and Klaff were sitting on the front bench sobbing, their massive shoulders shaking as they tried to stifle the sound with handkerchiefs the size of tablecloths.

As Erindil passed Lira to Korl and the couple took each other's hands, even the elf sniffled as he took his seat.

"Welcome, everyone," Rosie said, poking her head around Korl's massive form to be seen. "I'd like to open this celebration with a gnome hat ritual, but since you aren't gnomes and don't have hats to tie together, I suppose we'll skip straight to the vows."

Then Rosie recited some unusual weddings vows for the couple to repeat, Glen warbled more protests at being denied flowers to eat, and then the couple was kissing and walking back down the aisle.

"That was fast," Cali said to Sass as Glen trotted behind the newlyweds.

"Aye, a dwarf ceremony would take at least an hour. And that's if the couple are fast tunnelers."

Cali started to ask Sass to explain how tunneling was a part of a dwarf wedding ceremony but decided against it.

Once they'd all recessed to the back of the tavern, Vaskel slipped behind the bar and started pulling pints of ale. "It's time for a toast!"

Iris followed him, handing him clean tankards and slipping him sweet smiles as the couple worked together to pass out drinks to everyone. Cali took the pewter tankard that Sass handed her, but her attention was snagged by the front tavern door opening, bringing in a squall of snow along with a cloaked figure.

The archer instinctively reached for her bow, cursing that it wasn't on her back.

The lone figure tossed back her hood and shook out a mane of glossy, black curls. "I'm looking for the folks who delivered some hellkins to Eldu."

Val stepped forward, her shoulders squared. "That would be me."

"And me," Korl added.

Vaskel stepped from behind the bar. "Has something happened?"

The woman shrugged off her cloak to reveal leather pants tucked into high boots, a blousy shirt topped with a loose vest and a red sash cinching her waist. "You could say that."

Cali's mouth went dry as she eyed the stunning woman's clothing and thought about her favorite books. She pulled Lira closer to her and whispered, "Is she a pirate?"

* * *

Thank you for reading *Cauldrons, Charms & Chai*! If you enjoyed this cozy fantasy novel, you'll love the next book featuring Cali and the mysterious female pirate, *Potions, Pirates & Pie*.

* * *

This book has been edited and proofed, but typos are like little goblins that sneak in when we're not looking. If you spot a typo, please report it to: tlstoneauthor@gmail.com
Thank you!

Lira's Chai

Ingredients:

2 1/4 cups water
1 cinnamon stick
3 whole cloves
4 green cardamom pods, cracked open and deseeded
(throw seeds & pods in)
3 black peppercorns
1/2- inch fresh ginger, peeled and thinly sliced
3 black tea bags or substitute 3 tsp loose leaf black tea
1 cup whole or 2% milk
4 tsp sugar

Lira's Chai

Instructions:

Heat a medium saucepan over high heat. Add water, cinnamon stick,
cloves, cardamom pods, black peppercorns,
and ginger. Bring to a boil and add the tea bags or leaves.

Reduce the heat to medium-low and simmer gently for 7-10 minutes,
depending on how strong you'd like the tea and spices.
It will turn a deep burgundy color and reduce slightly.

Add milk and sugar and stir. Raise the heat to high (or allow the milk
to come to a boil on its own).

Reduce the heat to medium and simmer for another 5 minutes.
When ready to serve, raise the heat to high and allow it to come to
a rolling boil for 1-2 minutes.
Pour into cups through a strainer and add more sweetener, if desired.

Hot Cocoa Cookies

Ingredients:

1 cup melted butter (2 sticks)
½ cup cocoa powder
1 cup brown sugar
½ cup white sugar
2 large eggs
1 teaspoon vanilla extract
½ teaspoon salt
1 teaspoon baking soda
2 ¼ cups flour
14 marshmallows (not miniature)

Chocolate glaze:
8 oz. semisweet chocolate chips
3 Tablespoons butter
4 teaspoons milk
4 teaspoons honey (or corn syrup)

Cookies:

Melt two sticks of butter (1 cup) in the microwave. Combine melted butter and cocoa powder in a large mixing bowl or bowl of a stand mixer.
Stir until smooth.

Mix brown sugar and white sugar with the butter/cocoa mixture.
Add eggs and vanilla.
Mix in salt, baking soda, and flour.
Cover bowl with plastic and chill dough for 45 minutes-1 hour.
Preheat oven to 350 degrees.
Scoop dough onto parchment paper lined cookie sheets (2 Tbsp. size).

Bake cookies for 10 minutes. While cookies bake
cut marshmallows in half with scissors.

Place a marshmallow half (sticky side down) onto each hot cookie.
Place cookies back in the oven and bake an
additional 2-3 minutes (marshmallows should be slightly puffed).
DO NOT OVERBAKE MARSHMALLOWS.

Press each marshmallow down with the back of a spoon.

Let cool on a cookie sheet for a few minutes
then transfer to a wire rack to cool completely.

Hot Cocoa Cookies

Glaze:

Heat glaze ingredients in a microwave-safe bowl
for 30 seconds. Stir.

Heat for an additional 15-20 seconds. Stir until smooth and creamy.
If additional time is needed, do it in 10-second increments.

(You can use a double boiler or small saucepan over the stove
to melt the chocolate and glaze instead of a microwave.)

Drizzle glaze over cookies. Allow glaze to set (placing cookies
back into the refrigerator for 15-20 minutes will speed this up).

Also by T.L. Stone

Tusks, Tails & Teacakes

Sorcery, Swords & Scones

Solstice, Spice & Everything Nice (A Tiny Tale from the Tavern)

Cauldrons, Charms & Chai

Potions, Pirates & Pie

T.L. Stone is a cozy fantasy author who loves writing and reading about friends who become family, fantastical realms, and cozy moments where everything is right with the world. She likes her books and sweaters thick, her drinks sweet and hot, and her pastries buttery.

She's on a quest to make the perfect brownie, and her almond pound cake is swoonworthy. When she's not writing, you can find her cozied up to a crackling fire with a good book or planning her next travel adventure.

9 781962 806640